LANDFALL 231

May 2016

Editor David Eggleton
Founding Editor Charles Brasch (1909–1973)

Cover: Peter Peryer, Veil, 2015,
200 x 300 mm. Digital print.

Published with the assistance of Creative New Zealand.

OTAGO UNIVERSITY PRESS

CONTENTS

The Lord of Work, *Nick Ascroft* 4
Cruise Ship Day, *Shelley Arlidge* 6
A Line from Bruce Jenner, *Mark Young* 7
Beauty, *C.K. Stead* 8
A Continent Is Not an Island, *Jodie Dalgleish* 12
Koru, *Jessie Puru* 19
Clown of the Alps, *Liz Breslin* 20
Charms, *Claire Orchard* 22
Matilda, *Rachael Taylor* 24
Weekends, *Brian Turner* 31
This Woman I Met, *John Adams* 33
Doubtful Sound, *Judy O'Kane* 34
Waharoa, *Vaughan Rapatahana* 36
Sounds of Rimutaka, *L.E. Scott* 38
Aukati, *Antony Millen* 40
Why She Quit Queen at Night, *Carin Smeaton* 45
Amores, *Erik Kennedy* 46
ART PORTFOLIO, *Peter Peryer* 48
Researching Ali`i, *Leilani Tamu* 57
The Not Quite Full Moon, *Allison Li* 58
A Baby, *Rata Gordon* 60
And we have all been each other's mothers over countless lifetimes, *Victoria Broome* 61
Two poems, *Siobhan Harvey* 62
The Visit, *Ruth Arnison* 64
Every Family, *Sam Keenan* 65
Some Things About My Life, *Jillian Sullivan* 66
Prayer, *Johanna Emeney* 75
In which I defend our father's right to solitude, *Heather McQuillan* 77
My Father's Fingers, *Doc Drumheller* 79
Fire-walker, *Wes Lee* 80
From Benedictine Sonnets, *Koenraad Kuiper* 81
Time Trails, *Caoimhe McKeogh* 82

Sugar Town, *Madeline Reid* 87
The Stone in My Shoe, *Stephen Coates* 92
Mondegreen, *Helen Vivienne Fletcher* 95
A Modern Look at the Seven Deadly Sins, *Martha Morseth* 101
Anxiety, *Joanna Preston* 105
A Night with Strangers, *Owen Marshall* 106
From The Stone Women, *Christina Stachurski* 113
Gift, *Tom Weston* 121
Three 'Willow' Pattern Bowls, *Elizabeth Smither* 124
Paekakariki, At, To, From, *Piet Nieuwland* 125
Seven Haiku, *Bob Orr* 126
ART PORTFOLIO, *Saskia Leek* 128
Yes. Good., *Janet Charman* 137
Three Variations on 'The Red Wheelbarrow' by William Carlos Williams,
    Will Leadbeater 146
Matters of Accommodation, *Vivienne Plumb* 148
Middlemarch, *I.K. Paterson-Harkness* 152
Her Mountain Parents Meeting, *Elizabeth Welsh* 154
A View of the Canterbury Plains, *Robert McLean* 155
Inward, *Mary Macpherson* 157
An Extract from Work in Progress, *Bill Direen* 158
Two poems, *Ron Riddell* 160
From Skip to the End, *Victor Rodger* 165

    THE LANDFALL REVIEW

Landfall Review Online: Books recently reviewed 170
Andrew Dean on *The Back of His Head* by Patrick Evans 171
Kirstine Moffat on *The Chimes* by Anna Smaill 177
Thom Conroy on *Trifecta* by Ian Wedde 179
Jack Ross on *R.H.I.* by Tim Corballis 182
David Herkt on *The Fixer* by John Daniell 186
Elizabeth Heritage on *Credit in the Straight World* by Brannavan Gnanalingam 188
Max Oettli on *John Fields Signature Series 1975* 191

    LANDFALL BACK PAGE Mango-Tu, *Ngataiharuru Taepa* 208

NICK ASCROFT

The Lord of Work

I worked through lunch.
I worked through dinner, through the night and through breakfast.
I worked through an otherwise relaxing shower.

I worked through weekends and public holidays.
I worked on the Sabbath. I worked through Ramadan.
I worked through Kwanzaa.

I worked through 'Welcome to the Working Week' by Elvis Costello.
I worked through the Lou Reed song 'Don't Talk to Me about Work'.
I worked through 'This Woman's Work' by Kate Bush.

I paused only to make like I thought I was going to sneeze.
Then worked through the sneeze itself when it came.
I worked through the hiccups, the chickenpox and the manflu.

I worked through Tropical Cyclone Pam.
I worked through the Iranian nuclear deal.
I worked through the Tour de France.

I worked with my eyes closed.
I worked hands free.
I worked with ergonomic equipment and still developed epicondylitis.

I worked while I slept, like the Buddha.
I worked while I was not working, like the Zen Buddha.
I worked as I lay reading *As I Lay Dying* by William Faulkner.

I worked as I lay dying.
You can't work when you're dead.
But I'll work when I'm dead like Jesus, or Sisyphus.

SHELLEY ARLIDGE

Cruise Ship Day

The great white ship slows, stops
and turns, imperceptibly at first,
pivoting on the point of its anchor,
and settles, bow to stream of tide
like a white tern on a wild beach
with head tucked and neck feathers
just ruffling in the breeze.

Soon the tenders swing out and down,
their bellies pale under
orange domes, moving to the jetty
like ticks crawling on a horse,
gravid and ready to burst,
spilling out their offspring
in bright shirts and sunhats,
carrying credit cards and cash.

The ship dwarfs the hills.
People in the surrounding towns
supplicate as if to a great god.
Visitors come ashore
for tours, ice-creams, salads
and a floor that doesn't move.
In the afternoon they leave.
The ship shrinks, then disappears,
and the horizon's whole again.

MARK YOUNG

A Line from Bruce Jenner

The drop in Asian tourists
caused by the collapse of a
very large, dense interstellar
cloud means Facebook goes

down again & we end up looking at our city in a different way.
Recession looms over Eurozone,
tea sales fall in Russia, oil prices

slump below $40 per barrel. A
little short circuit in the wire is
an easy way to induce road-
kill. It is a maxim CEOs live by.

C.K. STEAD

Beauty

One: Like a bird
(for Kay)

Long ago, remember,
when we lived on the beach
at Takapuna, a Texan

teacher of maths bought a
fisherman's dizzy wife for
one thousand pounds—a good

price, equal to one year's
professional salary.
All three—the fisherman,

the Texan maths-man, the wife—
were pleased with the deal and
partied to celebrate.

We were there. I recall
the fact more clearly than
the party. Much wine was drunk,

and so, soon, were the drinkers.
There was a moon on the sea
right out to Rangitoto.

You were beautiful, and I
sang, as I could in those days
all the way home—like a bird.

Two: The telephone

The men he knew when young and worked with
were ten years older, sometimes twenty.
They envied him his beautiful wife and wondered
how he had won her, what was his secret.
He was clever but so were they, he wrote well
but they did too. He could stand on his hands on a table
his body horizontal slowly lifting
until his feet were over his head
but would a woman count that
more than a trick of balance?
    And would it affect her choice?
They talked about him, the buck with the beautiful wife
and joked about it. He was skinny,
and losing his hair.
       Life they concluded
was full of surprises and discrepancies.
It was like a telephone ringing
in an empty house and no one to answer.

Three: Terrible beauty

Yeats prayed his
daughter might be granted
'Beauty', but not

so much of it
she would drive suitors
mad, or herself

in the looking-glass.
Seeing her once
where the river

runs out from the
Lake of Innisfree
I thought she might

well have been
the plainest woman
in all Ireland

who'd lived a long
life with a famous
father's famous

and foolish
petition so patently
not granted.

Four: Not ever

We knew what we meant
—the lure, the lurch, the catch in the breath,
confusion of yearning and delight—
but couldn't agree on examples.

   'A morepork in the night,' she suggested.
'Yes—but no. Unvarying, repetitious.'
   'Some sunsets?' I didn't think so.
I wanted to suggest Strauss's four last songs
(ravishing!)—but knew she was a fan of Springsteen.

Shelley has a poem declaring his dedication
to an 'awful Loveliness', which seems almost as bad
as Willie's 'terrible beauty'.
   But Shelley's instance is a good one—
moonlight on a midnight stream.

Hannah Arendt wrote of 'the banality of evil'—
there's a banality of Beauty too:
Keats for example insisting it was Truth,
and that Truth was Beauty—the two big-name dummies
out-staring one another in a mirror.

There was a woman on a blog so beautiful
I wanted to put her into a poem,
but how would you do that?
      She was Australian,
a writer. No Marilyn Monroe,
a hazel-eyed brunette,
long pale face, fine mouth, and eyes
that looked right past me, away into the future
where I will never go, won't see, not ever.

Five: In Genoa

(where the B.V.M. is crowned
annually as the city's Queen)

Here the Mother of Jesus
is painted often as if
by a sceptic soul who works
in secret from a model

or a sentimentalist
whose vision ratifying
faith's most difficult demand
makes her a pretty Virgin.

Hail holy Queen do you hear
the streets of the city ring
with gratitude and praise for
your promised intercession

while the Ligurian Sea
whose beauty came before yours
and will outlast it teaches
only to trust what is so?

JODIE DALGLEISH

A Continent Is Not an Island

Before I left New Zealand, I often needed to walk a beach, for the shoreline, and the horizon line. They were demarcations I could follow, or trace with a finger, as a rite of accord and connection. And they were thresholds for a more speculative space, especially when sky was reflected in water that brought it to my feet.

I remember, on my last summer's Christmas morning, I went down to a beach, too early after losing sleep. There had been a glassy dawn tide that lay still over sand, sea and sky. Walking down to the end, I looked out to a small boat I saw suspended in its aerial bowl of sea-air, the silver mirror of its meniscus unclasping it, except for its wake, released.

Venice
In June, after packing my life of books into sixteen storage boxes, I took my honorary EU passport and headed, initially, to Venice to host the New Zealand exhibition at the Venice Biennale.

To find my way in the labyrinthine water city, I was eventually to learn, I must create an internal narrative of way-markers. These would help me not only to cope with the sudden and crazy reality of a Biennale-based endeavour, in the height of the summer season, but also to frame why, and in what way, I was suddenly there.

On arriving, I had the strange sensation of having not arrived, of having no impact on such an unlikely place, of having no purpose and no connection to myself, or others. Photographing barred entrances and their courtyards, while out on my first day, I come across a small bookshop, and go in. In poor Italian, I ask the young woman proprietor if she has English-language books about Venice and she puts Joseph Brodsky's *Watermark* and Italo Calvino's *Invisible Cities* into my hands.

In Brodsky's autobiographical *Watermark*, I start to feel a synchronicity with his description of his exclusion from the city's visage, of his loss of direction as a psychological category, and of sensing himself as some kind of compass. I also recognise Calvino's fabulist city in its fifty-five instances of one: his hidden cities, his cities of desire, his cities of memory. Essential as a course of water, says Brodsky who revisited Venice over seventeen winters, is the enquiry of what follows what, the run of a narrative.

    I am trying to find the only hardware store in Venice to buy nylon thread to tie together the handles of semi-automatic doors that have died due to handling and heat. And I am telling myself to remember to take the right-most turn when facing the door of the nearest of 149 churches, where I had previously taken the furthest left which took me, in the peak of the day, to the deadlock of Rialto. Then I am reminding myself to take the left at the corner of the narrow calle where I had sheltered with a press of others in an electrical storm under the restaurant awning that unceremoniously collapsed with the weight of torrential rain, and to remember the immediate right that opens to the only canal that will get me to the next sestiere, and to follow straight on from there.

    Waymarkers arise from a process of walking to find my way, running my fingertips over my experience through criss-crossing calli, as they also arise from a process of reading. Over time, I am forming a corporeal kind of text to witness a writer's explorations of the intricacies of a city, and the possible synchronous rhythm and fit (or not) of myself with it, in the 'flow of lymph', as Calvino puts it. Out there is a city Calvino describes in the words of Marco Polo, in which you might go out with a magnifying glass and hunt carefully to find somewhere that is a point no bigger than the head of a pin, and which, looked at enlarged, reveals details within details, blossoming like a city within a city until all the cities have bloomed out to a full-sized city and, at its heart, is the city yet to be discovered.

    In *Invisible Cities*, Polo's story becomes a journey through memory, more hopeful from 'so far away'. It contains the past like the lines of a hand, written into the lattice of its nooks and crannies, while it is always nostalgically linked to the desire of a dreamed-of city. It is a city of the living with a history of illusions and emotions of what could have been, as it is also, likewise, a city of the dead.

    On a day off, I take the public water boat to the Armenian exhibition, away from the crush, at the monastery on Isola San Lazzaro, which, since the eighteenth century, has also been a printing house at the centre of the Armenian culture and its diaspora. There, in a resonant stone-run room, I find the original print workshop, now a museum and archive of old blocks of type, presses, printing apparatus, maps and texts, and the site of Armenian-born filmmaker Nigol Bezjian's installation, *Witness.ed*.

Simultaneously sounding out the length of the writers' space are five videos, in each of which a non-English reader impresses importance upon the life and words of the late Armenian poet Daniel Varoujan, murdered in the Armenian genocide of World War I. Writer Marc Nichanian is first with his deliberation of Varoujan's 'To the Cilician Ashes', the landmark poem that voiced the destruction of the 1909 progroms across the Mediterranean Cilician plain with the metaphorical act of inscribing a tomb elsewhere. As Nichanian recounts the poet's lines, he considers the poet-as-mourner and poetry as a medium of mourning, within an assembly of poets all speaking at once.

For me, digital recorder in hand, *Witness.ed* proposes a space of both philological impotence and possibility. Only a few months after the sudden death of my mother, I write words towards a poem, later read into the played-back burble of that recorded room. Recording again, I speak, almost unheard, of its blocks of type that take ink at their end, for the weight of press and the promise of maps and production and direction; of the writer's tools and display of switches, screws, springs, bolts, pistons, pulleys, tapes, trays, cogs, wires, moulds, handles, keepers, stands and boards; and my inability, still, to bury her.

Luxembourg
I left Venice with a co-mingling of relief and regret, as I was escaping and losing an extraordinary city. Standing on deck to see the last of her, I could turn and look forward to making a central continental residence, to write, and to rest.

I watched from my plane's take-off as water disappeared for vastness of land, as if a network of calli could lead me, through one village and another, to a charming abode.

That night, in the new rental apartment, I made my first attempt at liking the new bed. Sweltering, I got up to walk around three small, empty and featureless rooms. I stood at the window onto the road, troubled by the loud flow of cars passing, and the cargo planes close overhead. In a state of stasis, I was unable to go back to bed, and lay down to pass an hour on the cool, hard, tiled floor.

Paris
Surrounded by the rest of Europe, in Luxembourg, I took a two-hour train to Paris. There, where I could hear and speak the accent I learned by rote in school, I hoped to immerse myself in the experience of les langues, in the process of moving words and ideas back and forth, to sound out fully their concurrence, and the gaps of their misconnections.

Like the French, I would not use the word 'langage' for 'language', but the more hopefully associated word langue, which translates as 'tongue'. More bodily, this 'langue' links a speaker to words that are sur la bout de la langue, on the tip of the tongue. More active, it invites one to parler la langue couramment, to speak a language fluently—in the 'current', 'flow' and 'stream' of the root of courant and, in the related run of courir, to make a course, and take a chance. Essentially, in its fluency I could relate the most fundamental of verbs, 'to be', as in être au courant de ('be aware of things').

Wanting to find a key text that will link me to being in Paris, I take one line of the underground Métro to Clignancourt and make my way to the city's largest and oldest flea market, the Marché aux Puces. Criss-crossing the blaring traffic flow of a few main arterials in the slipstream of jay-walking locals, and passing a proliferation of hawkers and stalls, I find myself at the Marché Dauphine: a skylighted, two-storey pavilion of 6000 square metres, and only the first (I was to find out later) of its fifteen markets.

In Le Carré des Libraires, which collects across the second floor the rare books, photographs, postcards, engravings and lithographs of 120 Dauphine marchands, one bookseller introduces me to another until one takes the oversized Paris du temps perdu from his shelf. 'Proust,' he says—in such a deep r-throated way I shake my head as if I have not heard of the man—is there excerpted alongside Eugène Atget's photographs of the lost, and oldest, part of Paris.

Opening the book, I study lines from the first volume of Proust's lifelong novel, À la recherche du temps perdu, laid out as verse in its introduction:

> Mais, quand d'un passé ancien rien ne subsiste,
> après la mort des êtres, après la destruction des
> choses, seules, plus frêles mais plus vivaces, plus
> immatérielles, plus persistantes, plus fidèles, l'odeur
> et la saveur restent encore longtemps, comme des
> âmes, à se rappeler, à attendre, à espérer, sur la
> ruine de tout le reste, à porter sans fléchir, sur leur
> gouttelette presque impalpable, l'édifice immense
> du souvenir.

From the first line, there is a loss of what was there before, a death (*la mort*) of being (with *être*, the verb 'to be'). For me, there is the destruction of things, followed by the word *seules*, alone, followed by the frail but living, the immaterial but persistent, the subject with fidelity that remains, like a call of infinitives: *à se rappeler* (to remember), *à attendre* (to wait), *à espérer* (to hope), in the structure, or edifice, of memory.

Not long after, I return to the strange call and indeterminacy of that run-on text, considering the translation of Scott Moncrieff and its revision by Terence Kilmartin. In their versions, as is standard, the infinitive—described as 'to + the unconjugated form of the verb'—is made into the most understandable, yet less emphatic 'remembering', 'waiting' and 'hoping'. Falling short, for me, also, is the way smell and taste, operating like souls (*les âmes*), become the owners of these infinitive actions.

As in my first encounter, I am not willing to give up the indefinable way in which the identification of Proust's subject, which persists, and is calling, is ambiguous, open—perhaps like memory itself—to the act of searching closely. Because of the late call of the infinitive that comes after the death of the living, aloneness and persistence, and the fact that the first verb to be named is the pronominal *se rappeler*, with its reflexive pronoun, I, as the reader, become more implicated and involved. Beginning a verse of my own, then, to worry *les langues* and this proclivity, I make an approximation where the more frail yet long-lived, more immaterial, more persistent, more constant, lingering scent and taste, like the self, is to call back, to wait, to hope, upon the ruin of everything left, to carry an infinitesimal trace, into the immense edifice of memory.

Venice

Going back in winter, I was unsure of my ability to recall its calli, but as soon as my feet hit the paving stones of the Santa Luca railway station I was on my way to our rented apartment, which I knew to be around the corner from the bar that I was told, when I was first unable to find it, was next to the Biennale's *Dansaekhwa* exhibition.

But my reacquaintance is interrupted when I wake to be told by my husband that, the night before, Paris was under terrorist attack and a state of emergency has been declared. I keep asking for the known facts of it over and over again. Assault rifles, suicide belts, explosives, execution style. Six locations across the city where people gather: a sports stadium, an intersection, a corner, two restaurants, a concert hall. The act is, then, unclaimed, and we sit exchanging stunned phrases about its violence, and its proximity.

I had been reading Georges Perec's *Tentative d'épuisement d'un lieu parisien* ('An Attempt at Exhausting a Place in Paris'), in which he describes in detail, over one weekend, the intricacies of the Place Saint-Sulpice, as a means of locomotion and traction, as degrees of bodily determination and motivation. And, only days before that, I had noted an appealing, but now removed, excerpt from his *Species of Spaces*: 'this is how space begins, with words only, signs traced on the blank page. To describe space: to name it, to trace it, like those portolano makers who saturated the coastlines with the names of harbours, the names of capes, the names of inlets …'

Perhaps instinctively, we get onto the water and go to the small Lagoon island of Burano, known over centuries for the craft of its lace. It is a very different season to my last visit. There are not the same throngs pressing their hands to souvenirs, yet we wander around the perimeter, as if pacing out the distance of some private geography.

On the boat back at dusk, leaning over the sheen of the water, I take photographs, a plethora of records of sea merging with sky.

What a contrast to the boats of armed police patrols on the Grand Canal the next morning.

Luxembourg

After our return, through heightened security checks, I spend a couple of shuffling days, tidying my 'writing room'.

I remove plastic wrap and unfurl a roll of tracing paper with its smooth pearlescence and touch of tissue. Not too far away from it is *Paris du temps perdu* and I leaf through its images to consider some of those most familiar to me: the window display with the chair and its miniature atop a chiffonier, a cobbler's shelves of polished boots, a trestle table in a corner with stacks of printing and books, the ornate turn of a stairwell, the thin shadows of plane trees on a maison. Sitting at my desk, I start to trace the first, attending to the mark of graphite, pressing my fingers to the blank page, to my line and the work underneath.

Aotearoa

Aotearoa is the island I reach back to, but not the *terra firma* I look out from. I can't walk a shoreline and my horizon line is lost, given up in favour of a continent of space I wish to cross, connect and articulate.

Soon after arriving in Europe, in a room of Venice's Museo Correr, I came across a seventeenth-century globe tipped on its axis so as to propose, in big letters, the still-unknown domain of 'Terre Arti'. On either side, and across a narrow-to-wider piece of ocean, is a coastline, a familiar meandering and traceable shoreline with innumerable possibilities for landings. It consists of nooks and crannies along the run of a pen, or a pencil, while it disappears, unfinished, off the curves of the sphere, as if to welcome travellers to the indefinite expanse of its hypothetical name.

If Terre Arti exists for me, it is one of geography and incidence, where space allows movement and experience across a new locus of points linked, like Perec's space of language, by the portolano-makers' alphabet, in a 'continuous ribbon of text'. Where I am now, I construct a network of places, and of memory and affection, as a process of work, as a story of practice.

JESSIE PURU

Koru

```
                        It is the curl y
                      our tongue makes as
                     the Rs take off in flight like
                      rererangi –      then flattens
                       out to cle      ar your thro
                       at, prepa       ring your l
                       ungs to be filled    with appr
                        oval from the tup    una – it is
                          fronds slouchi     ing away
    from the d              amp, k        eeping its
    driest parts ins                      ide to fight
    against that chilled                  outer spine
          each one contains a little    blurb hidden
            in its chest that will likely never open to
                be read – a secret in a closed fist
```

LIZ BRESLIN

Clown of the Alps

Who wouldst not leave him in his wandering
To seek for treasure in the jewelled skies,
Albeit he soared with an undaunted wing?
—Edgar Allan Poe, 'Sonnet to Science'

and there they were, pulling hot-air exits from off Easy Rider
when they caught clowns keening from home—
keeaa keeaa—across the white
of the slopes, byte between a gap in the pumped-out tracks on the blue

toothed earpiece. *Sweet. It's what they call*
habitat, innit. That's natural, innit. Pass us another
Monteiths. They're sitting in the Cheeky Kea, ten runs down now, sun
blaring on their stories. Their skies,

jewelled in the racks, done for the day, flown from the UK to swoop
the slopes out of season. Lonely,
really, ruling the world, is what
no one ever says. *keeaa keeaa*, hopping low and ringed and free.

J comes hopping for the sour-cream
leftovers, insistent, persistent little jumped-up fuck he is.
Beak deep, white, milky—who needs to rip back fat out of sheep? Fast-food
frenzied, J can open cartons,

wrestle rubber weather-stripping. You leave him in his wandering,
you lose. *Hey, dick, be vigilant of your things.*
This year's goggles, tapered jacket.
Catch a flash of orange underfeather, J assaults another

packet. Squat, hops, mossy, static.
Why bother undaunting your wing when it's all laid on here? *We'll see them fly sometime. Come on, one more lap. Laters J, seeya.* Never call your last run. *keeaa keeaa*

CLAIRE ORCHARD

Charms

Driving along Main Street the old places dangle,
unpolished, from a tacky tarmac chain:
the squat, grey-rock women's hospital,
the chipped and faded boards of our grandparents'
ex-state bungalow. The Baptist Church's cut-glass angles
now The River of Life Centre and, opposite,
my once-boyfriend's cubazoid, sunset brick-and-tile
studded with net-curtained windows.

The centrepiece of the collection, the high school, has
sustained some major alterations. The maths prefabs
have gone. The science labs, solid concrete blocks
that surely should have stood monument forever,
have been razed, entirely replaced by a rectangle-cut gem
of emerald grass set with three saplings.

Doubling back, I drive through the front gates
that, according to the sign, should be locked by now.
But tonight the carpark is full of vehicles;
there's something going on in the hall. Parent–teacher
conferences? Careers night? At a crawl I complete
the circuit, passing the marae, the special needs unit;
both seem to have shrunk. At the exit, the mural
on the road-facing wall is unchanged,
its violently erupting volcano still showering
that unnamed wahine in ash and steam, her face
still wearing that vague, unfinished look.

Pulling up to the roundabout there's a faint figure
looming in the dusk, a teenage girl running
in front of my car. Her mate hesitates, looking
directly at me. I smile and wave at her and, although
she still seems unsure, she goes anyway.
I pass them, still running, pleated tartan skirts
flying. And then there's those god-awful imitation windmills,
a final faded pair of geegaws, smaller from this angle.

RACHAEL TAYLOR

Matilda

People don't like me, not the way they like my sister Matilda. I don't mind—no, really I don't. It's just a fact. Matilda has a kind of people magnetism, it's hard to define—she's just her pure, open self at every moment. She doesn't hold any part of herself back and maybe that's what puts people at ease. She never dwells on the past or thinks too much about the future; things work out for her. I'm pretty lucky because me and Matilda are close like best friends; close in age too, she being only eleven months older than me.

Matilda's tall, around five-nine, and beautiful too, so people notice her. She gets her long legs and olive skin from Dad's side. She's got wild frizzy hair, which she hates but everyone else loves. Growing up we used to joke all the time about how different we looked from one another. We joked that Mum had jumped the fence and done it with our old neighbour, Mr Johnson, and then she had me. We joked, but sometimes I wondered for real.

Last summer Matilda's presence took on an altogether brighter extreme; everyone seemed dazzled by her. The population in the Bay doubles over the summer and we were having a pretty social time, our place being so close to the beach. We had parties and BBQs and Matilda was always there in the spotlight. It was like Matilda knew a secret that none of us others could figure. People would open up to her about all sorts of things going on in their lives—problems usually, or some kind of trouble, and she'd sit with them and talk it through. She didn't exactly tell them what to do; she just helped them to see the answers for themselves. She could have charged for that kind of expertise!

It got to be that me and our friend Tom made a joke about it. We've got private jokes about nearly everything, me and Tom, like a comedy duo. We always say, 'That's one for the notebook!' (the notebook being an imaginary book we write all our great comedy moments in so we don't forget them). The one we had about Matilda over the summer was this: any time we were stuck in a bad situation or feeling mean-spirited about someone we'd say, 'What would Tilda do?' The answer would always be something brilliant or kind-hearted or generous—the very opposite of what would come naturally to me or Tom. And it was unbelievable—if we followed through it would always work out. 'What would Tilda do?' Just like she was Jesus. We even told her about it. She didn't mind; she knew we weren't meaning it in a nasty way. Matilda was good-natured about everything.

Matilda had been living back in the Bay about a month and she'd met a guy pretty much straight away. You could tell he was infatuated with her and he was an all right kind of guy, too. He bought her presents and took her on dates and paid for everything and it was pretty clear that he was aiming to lock her down, marriage and kids and all that. He was in a big kind of hurry.

People told her, 'Tilda, that Blair's a really top guy. You're so lucky to meet someone who treats you so good. You deserve it.'

And Matilda would say, 'Yeah, totally,' in a way that didn't sound convincing at all.

The thing about Blair was that he was always wanting to make her try new things, like dinners in restaurants where they set the food on fire in front of you or serve a whole fish with its eyes still sticking out of its head. One time she came home and told me they'd eaten a meal that cost more than her week's wages! She said the plates of food were so tiny that she was still hungry and we made peanut butter on toast and laughed about it.

Blair took her for a ride in a helicopter and a cruise on a yacht in the harbour. Then one day they went scuba diving. The Dive Centre was on the Esplanade not far from the Kebab Shack where me and Tilda worked. We knew Darren, the owner—he was a good guy, a regular customer—and his wife's nieces, Kat and Leah, worked part time with us, too.

Me and Tom sat on the rocks and watched as Tilda, Blair and Darren walked into the sea like aliens in their wetsuits, masks and tanks. Their heads disappeared beneath the surface of the sea. We watched shadows of clouds passing over the water, waves breaking, seagulls calling each other names. It seemed like ages they were down there in that unnatural way and then they resurfaced, heads, bodies, legs, right down to their flippers, and they moved awkwardly up the beach towards us.

Something happened after that. Matilda was changed. Diving was different for her in a way she could love. She couldn't get enough of it.

'You wouldn't believe how incredible it is down there,' she said. 'It's a soft, mesmerising rainbow world. I feel so alive and free; so happy.'

Me and Tom looked at each other, thinking this was one for the notebook.

'Are you sure you haven't got that thing that divers get?' I said. 'You're acting pretty dizzy.'

'Nitrogen narcosis,' said Tom.

'Not funny,' Matilda said, but she was smiling. 'Ange, you should come diving with me and Darren some time. Honestly, it's amazing, you have no idea. Darren's promised to take me out to the shipwreck one day soon.'

'No thanks. I'm happy with my feet on solid ground,' I said.

Matilda's relationship with Blair didn't last much longer than a few months. They fought all the time and what they fought about was the fact that she didn't feel the same way for him as he did about her. It was driving him crazy. When he couldn't make her love him through his generosity and devotion he looked for ways to hurt her back instead. She didn't put up with that for long. She told me he'd verbally abused her, criticised her. He'd said she was cold and heartless. It was a shock for her to hear this, but only a minor one really, because she didn't have any real feelings for him to begin with. That was the first time I ever thought less of my sister Matilda. I felt sorry for that guy Blair because I knew exactly what it was like to love someone in the worst kind of way and not be loved back.

Matilda didn't lose any of her glow after that breakup. She never mentioned the guy. I'd ask, 'How you going with that? Feeling ok?'

'Course, Ange!' she'd say. 'That Blair turned out to be a nasty piece of work and better I saw it sooner than later.' But there was something she wasn't saying. I just knew it.

First Matilda's car was defaced: the tyres slashed and the windows smashed in. *Ho-Slut-Bitch* was spray-painted across the side.

I couldn't believe it. 'Not Blair?' I said.

'They must have got the wrong car,' Tilda said quietly.

'Yeah,' I said, feeling relieved for her. 'Why would anyone do that to *you*?' But that wasn't the end of it.

'How did your sister like her car?' Kat asked that afternoon at work.

'You?' I said. 'But why?'

'Go ask your bitch-sister.'

We went for a walk on the beach after that shift. I told Matilda what Kat had said and she defended her. Matilda could only see the good in people.

'They've had a shitty life,' she said. 'Some of the things I know about them ...' She stopped walking and stared out at the sea.

'Like what?' I prompted her. 'What about them?'

Matilda was distracted. 'Okay, just promise you won't spread this?'

I promised and she told, and I thought maybe what she said went a way to explain why they messed up her car. Perhaps I needed to give it further consideration. That kind of information is like a burning stone in your stomach.

'Tom,' I said, the next time I saw him. 'So, Kat and Leah's mum is in jail.'

'So what?' he said.

'So, they were in foster care for a bit. Didn't work out; that's why they live with Darren and his wife and kids now.'

I'd broken a promise to Matilda but I knew it wouldn't go any further. I needed something of consequence to share with Tom, something more than our jokes and play, something serious or precious or powerful just between the two of us. If I'd expected reassurance from him or even interest, I didn't get it. 'Maybe that's why they're so mean.' I said desperately. 'It was them who vandalised Matilda's car.'

'*What?* Why?'

And it was then I realised I still didn't actually know.

It didn't take long to get to the truth. Matilda was too excited to keep it to herself. She wanted everyone to know, but that was impossible. Matilda must have had some idea of the danger but she trusted me. As soon as she said it, I wished she hadn't.

'I've been seeing a guy, Ange. I'm in love.' She had never used the L word before. 'I've been wanting to tell you so bad, but ...' She was looking straight at me, her eyes flicking around searching for something. Loyalty? Permission?

'It's Darren.'

'Who's Darren?'

'*Darren* Darren. From the Dive Centre.'

'No,' I said. What she said broke hard rules we both knew and counted on. 'He's married with little kids.'

'I didn't mean to fall in love with him. God, of course not! You know me. I would never intentionally set out to hurt anyone that way.' Matilda looked at me with all the sincerity in the world. 'I love him and he loves me.'

'But how can you be sure?'

'I just am. I feel it,' she said.

I couldn't believe it. I worried about Matilda's certainty. She seemed to have lost all reason.

Matilda was unashamed of her love for Darren and believed that its power and purity answered for her moral disgrace. She spoke about love like she had invented it and needed to convince me of its value and its intensity, as if love was something I could never understand.

I barely recognised her any more. In her state of delirium no one else mattered, all consequences were ignored. She was consumed by her circumstances, over her head and oblivious to the risk. She was beyond help.

I was the only person Matilda could talk to, besides Darren himself, though by now it was common knowledge. Darren had left his wife and family and was sleeping at the Dive Centre. Matilda was branded a home-wrecker. Tension between Matilda and Darren's nieces at the Kebab Shack was unbearable. She quit and went to work in a gift store in the village. The question 'What would Tilda do?' had stopped being funny. Nothing in her life was very flash now. No one treated her with admiration or came to her for advice. She took walks on the beach and stared at the water. She visited Darren at the Dive Centre but she no longer went diving.

We had both stopped socialising in the Bay. Tilda's all-consuming love for Darren was a complete rejection of all other men. Tom left town: I was gutted; Matilda barely even noticed. Before the affair, to be by Tilda's side, even in her shadow, was a privilege. Now it was a cold and disappointing place to be.

All through the summer Matilda looked for a solution to her problem. She spent every moment consumed by figuring out what should be done, looking at the situation from all angles … Something was getting in the way of her happiness. Darren wouldn't give up on his family and the last thing Matilda ever wanted was to be the cause of pain to his wife and kids. That was what she couldn't stand. She knew it was too late to fix the past so she started to think about the bigger picture. She was looking hopefully to a future where she would be part of the family and they would all just have to accept it. She would be his children's step-mum and they would be the half-siblings of her and Darren's future offspring. Eventually people would recognise that she and Darren were soul mates and in it for the long haul. Given enough time, everything would be okay.

I had my doubts. Even if they could make it work and down the line people forgave her, could she really forgive herself? Could a relationship survive, let alone thrive, when its beginnings were so destructive? I raised these questions but I was only a sounding board now. Any concerns I had were nothing more than ripples on the surface of her latest resolution. Which was simple: they had to begin immediately to be out together in public as a couple, to be open and proud of the love they shared. This was the way forward, the beginning of their honest life together. Darren was to meet us at the pub where we would celebrate Matilda's sense of renewed clarity.

There was a band playing that night and the place was busy with locals and visitors to the Bay. I was glad of the company of strangers; we both felt the hostility of those who knew and disapproved of her.

'They just don't know the truth,' she said. 'When Darren gets here and stands up for me, he'll put them straight, they'll all see then.'

Kat and Leah stood at the bar hating us. I didn't care about them. What could they do in a place like this? We sat at a table on the far side, close to the band. It felt good to think of nothing, to have the thoughts pushed out of my head by the amplified music. But Matilda stayed close to me all the same. It was like she knew what was coming. Rules had been broken, penalties had to be paid. That was the only possibility as Kat and Leah saw it.

Matilda was pulled backwards off her chair by her hair, upending our table and shattering glass. Her face was pushed hard to the floor by the hand still tangled in her hair, and there followed several swift kicks to her stomach. These lithe and confident actions were accompanied by aggressive words I couldn't hear over the band. Matilda was passive, expectant. She kept her arms wrapped protectively around her head, she didn't fight back. She formed a fetal coil, a strange and disturbing posture for her long, athletic body, and she stayed like that even when it was over, like she was in shock or maybe she expected more to come. It happened so fast the band didn't even stop playing. I pulled Matilda into my arms and saw that there was a bleeding gash in her swollen cheek—a perfect new moon the size of a bottle cap.

Maybe Darren turned up that night, maybe he didn't. We had to leave straight away to get Tilda's face stitched up. In the days following the attack he moved back in with his wife and kids. 'Just for now,' he told Matilda. 'Just till things settle down.'

Six months on, the scandal hasn't tarnished my sister Matilda. Maybe it's even made her reputation stronger, her lovability greater and more relatable. Even with that crescent scar on her face Matilda is still beautiful. I'm the only one who notices she isn't quite as self-assured as she used to be. Around here there are still plenty of guys lining up to be with her. She's not taking any of them up on it though. She's waiting for Darren to leave his wife for good. He promised he would. She's still convinced their love is the real thing; other people would be lucky to ever find that kind of happiness.

BRIAN TURNER

Weekends

They hammer   they saw   they mow
they dig and weed   they wed
someone or other for better
rather than worse though it doesn't
always work out that way
when heartlands are heartless

But for now they mow
it's the song of the weekend
the world's at their feet
for this is a civilised place
and we believe in grass

A sunglassed babe pilots a ride-on
and across the road
a mother of two
pushes something less superior
back and forth
on the roadside verge

When the mowers stop
you can hear trilling again
melodies in the shrubs and trees
and tulips like goblets full of sunlight
shine in gardens entrusted to us

Who knows   impermanence
may not be permanent after all
if you find time to take stock

think of what a place could be
when it's not what we possess
that counts most
but what we are possessed by

JOHN ADAMS

This Woman I Met

Tells me she has four hives already,
a good start,
and she's been planting manuka
up and down the valley; says she dreams
of a hundred stonkin' little hives
hidden there, primed to discharge
a barrage
of bees. Their lazy hum will ruffle
the declivity of the valley
and the syrup will seep all the way
down to Te Matuku Bay
and sweeten the sea. A woman like that,
you can understand.

JUDY O'KANE

Doubtful Sound

If you love something, set it free,
you'd said, as we kayaked over
the glacial water, dolphins diving
under our boats, their breath

like steam irons.
If it doesn't come back,
hunt it down and kill it,
you'd said.

You don't remember that
when I come back
and we pull off our wetsuits
in the rain, our skin

a landing strip
for sandflies.
An echo calls across
the Sound. We see the tail

slapping the surface
like a huge paddle: the whale.
Later, two black eyes
meet mine in the dark.

Was it a kiwi? Did it sound
like this? you ask, fumbling
through your backpack
for a CD, but I can't identify it:

I'm not fluent in birdsong.
Your face falls; you say
it must have been
a possum.

VAUGHAN RAPATAHANA

Waharoa

this death thing
is a skulking cur
l o i t e r i n g
just   beyond
every door.

waiting for our wahine inside,
'*nō hea koe e hoa?*' I asked him
outside the lone latrine
Waharoa had to offer
adrift its weather-beaten
weatherboards
f u m b l i n g   a l o n g   the   street.

'Rotorua,' he said,
'just taking my sister home,'
as I traced his flicker
at the coffin
lumped in back
of the old stationwagon.

'picked her up from the airport,' he offered,
like a ruined lolly.

'from Australia?' I mused out loud.

'Perth,' he abridged.

'kāore he kupu mo koe e hoa,'
was the best I could do,
& the air tensed itself
in mute empathy.

when we drove off,
my wife asked, 'was that a hearse?'
as I beeped deep the horn
to his fatigued flourish
&
steering elderly,
noted more *urupā*
than I'd ever seen before,

on our way back
home to feed
the dog.

---

nō hea koe e hoa (where are you from, mate?)
kāore he kupu mo koe e hoa (not a word for you, mate)
urupā (burial ground)

L.E. SCOTT

Sounds of Rimutaka

The life noises are different here
the way people talk and listen
the way they walk and look but don't look
waiting for the misspoken word
the misplaced look
nuances are everywhere
a slight can lie dormant for light-years
blood-letting comes in a flash
didn't see nothin'
didn't hear nothin'

The life noises are different here
some mornings you wake
and the sounds of despair
would crush your soul
there are rituals every survivor must find
some turn to a newfound god
some bathe themselves with anger
some huff and puff to be king of the zoo
some are tumbleweeds in the desert
dancing with imaginary music just above their heads
some are deadly quiet
lost in the frozen frames
of their last living memories

The life noises are different here
the sound of keys that lock but do not open
it drinks the soul
it dries the blood

it reddens the eyes
it curls the tongue
the sound of uncertainty
time zone of the unknown
nothing is real but the moment

ANTONY MILLEN

Aukati

Don't go with them, my son. I'm telling you, you do not want to cross that line.

When Daddy moved here from Whakatane, I wasn't the only new kid in Urupuia. There was this other boy, Chris, who had come down from Auckland to live with his nan for the summer. Just like your mate Matiu does. Lots of kids live with their nans sometimes.

Chris had it different to me though. He had lots of whānau here—I mean heaps. All his cousins lived here and he had some pretty mean uncles around the place too, looking after him if he needed it. Not like me—I only had Dylan, but Dylan didn't stay.

Dylan was like your friend Tom. He was the tallest guy in our little gang on this side of the river and the oldest too. He looked out for me straight away when I arrived so I was all good. We used to hang out along the river and throw stones at the boys on the other side.

You know where the big rock is up from the bridge? That was a good place for throwing stones because there were plenty about the place and we had higher ground.

The other side got into it too. We used to taunt each other like mad, say some really horrible stuff. One time, I called this joker a gearbox cos his last name was Cairboss. He still has that nickname I reckon. But we used to come up with all sorts of wicked stuff.

And no one ever really got hurt either. I took a couple of stones to the head and nailed this one fella with a pinecone, but that was probably the worst that happened—lots of tears, but lots of laughs too. No one ever crossed the river. It was like an unwritten rule that we never crossed the river to have real fights or anything like that.

Except at the grove. Do you know where that is? Course you do. It's just down from where the Whakaroau meets the Wainui and you already know about the aukati up the Whakaroau.

Well, we knew about the aukati when we were kids too. We knew that no one was meant to go up there because an old Māori chief had placed an aukati on the Whakaroau. You're right, they said the line was between two enormous kahikatea trees on either side of the stream.

Do you know why he did that? It was before the railway was completed. The government planned to run the line through the chief's area and he'd heard about other urupā that were dug up for the rail. He wasn't having that. So he put an aukati on there and woe to anyone who crossed it.

For engineering reasons the railway line was diverted to where it is now—but the old man never lifted the aukati. Did you know that stream used to be a much larger river? No one knows why it dried up, but you used to be able to pilot a waka up there. The old pā hasn't had people on it for almost a hundred years, but the aukati is still there. Before you, the only person I'd ever heard talk about going past it was Chris, but Dylan stopped him.

I haven't been down to the grove since high school, but I imagine it's the same as it was then. We all used to climb trees there and it was the only place where we crossed over cos that's where the river narrowed and the trees reached so far out we could step onto a branch on the other side. No matter what kind of fights our gangs had, we didn't let those keep anyone from a cool thing like that.

I was the bomb at it and I reckon that was one of the reasons Dylan kept inviting me back to hang out with them. Chris was good at it too, but he didn't need to be invited. He had two cousins in our group so he just showed up one day and never left, even though he was a mean bugger right from the start. He used to do things like trip girls on the school bus and swing puppies in woolsacks. One day, when I told them all I was going home in the middle of our game of rounders, he pushed me into a stack of firewood. But he didn't do much when Dylan was around.

Then Dylan stopped hanging out with us. Once he got his licence that was the last we saw of him. No more biking around the sawmill or the quarry for him. Things didn't change right away, but I remember the day when Chris first brought his cousin Tayla to the grove.

We'd never had a girl hang out with us before. It was like another one of those unwritten rules. We didn't like it. It was Chris's idea to take her up to the rock and taunt the others across the river. Tayla had a wicked arm and she beaned one fella right in the eye with a stone. It wasn't good.

The other side threatened us, and it was more intense than usual. We just wanted to leave it alone, but Chris wouldn't let up. He answered back with all sorts of things, even promised to take out the guy's other eye.

The next time we got together was at the grove and the other gang was there too except for the wounded kid. Nobody said anything at first, but Chris jumped into the tree on our side of the river and made his way to the end of the branch.

There was another fella already there—Henare, I think his name was. Chris wouldn't let him pass and told him they weren't allowed over any more. Henare was pretty angry and yelled back, but Chris reached over and shoved him, nearly knocked him out of the tree. It scared the fella and he backed off. The boys all yelled from the other side, but took off when Chris crossed over and promised to take them all on by himself.

From the other side of the river, he called out to us, 'It's all ours now, boys!' I'd never seen such a broad grin.

So we played there some more during the summer, but we started to get a bit bored. We hadn't seen the other boys in a week and we were annoyed by Tayla always being there. She and Chris started talking to each other by themselves a lot more, hanging out in the trees or on the other side, sometimes disappearing into the bush for a while. It was weird.

It was Bailey's idea that someone should say something to him and it was Wiremu's idea that that someone should be me, which was a stupid idea cos I was so new. But without Dylan, someone had to step up, I guess.

In the end I didn't have to do it. Wiremu's house was closest to the grove and when I arrived he was already arguing with Chris. It was weird how it happened. Mu must have had a gutsful, cos he was having a good go at him, telling him he was sick of Tayla hanging around and how Chris had ruined the grove by chasing the others off.

It got pretty heated. I won't tell you exactly what Wiremu said about Chris and Tayla in the bushes, but just as he said it, Tayla arrived. He must have hit the nail on the head cos she burst into tears and ran away. Then Chris punched Mu in the stomach, so Tayla wasn't the only one crying.

I've never seen fire in a person's eyes, but Chris's were pretty hot. He yelled at us and stomped his feet. He told us the grove was all his now, and he was putting an aukati there so we'd better not cross it. We just let him go and checked on our mate.

We were scared to go back to the grove, and we didn't see Chris around any more either. We didn't have video games in those days so we had to find other things to do—bullrush mostly.

Summer came to an end and we had to go back to school. We talked about Chris and where he'd got to. Bailey said he might have left town, gone back to Auckland, but we weren't sure. Smaller kids in the neighbourhood said they'd seen him walking towards the river. None of them wanted to go there because they'd heard it was cursed. I still laugh at that. It was me who started calling Chris 'Curse' after he fobbed us off. Wiremu thought he'd seen him headed that way once, but it was dark so he wasn't sure.

It never sat right with me that we'd lost everything that summer. First I'd lost my best friend, then my best enemies, then my best climbing trees. I said we should go back to the grove, but the boys all said it was time to go back to school anyway. Rugby season was starting. It was getting dark earlier.

So I went by myself. Remember, I was much older than you are now. I went when I thought it was safest—on a sunny Sunday afternoon after church.

We used to get to the grove from behind Wiremu's back paddock. You probably get there from the quarry track, eh? Our way was quicker, but we had to scale some fences and cut through some blackberry. I loved it and felt more excited than afraid the closer I got.

Chris wasn't there. I'd never had the grove to myself before and had a great old time climbing the pukatea by myself and swinging from the willow trees. I didn't cross over the river straight away but when I tried to, I saw that something had changed since we'd been there.

Someone had chopped the branches off. Chris, no doubt. I could see the hack marks he left behind. He must have used some rusty old hatchet. The bugger had left the cuttings strewn along the banks. He'd planted some in the ground like some kind of hunting trophies for his little den.

I climbed down and waded across the shallowest bit to pull one of them out, and took it with me when I climbed to the top of the bank. I looked back across the river and realised there really was nothing to fear. For weeks we'd stayed away because of some egg. We'd let him ruin the rest of our summer. And that's when I did a stupid thing.

I thought about Chris's aukati, how it was some kind of phantom bogeyman, and I started thinking the other aukati must be the same. I pictured myself returning to the guys and telling them it was all good—not only was the grove ours again, but we could have the Whakaroau too.

So I headed up to where the Whakaroau meets the Wainui. I had no idea how far up the aukati was, but it was a brilliant Sunday afternoon and glory awaited me.

I know you won't think this is true, but this is exactly how it happened. The further up that stream I went, the darker it got, and it wasn't because of clouds or trees. Whenever I'd look up, the sun was still there with nothing blocking it, but when I looked down it was dark. I'm not lying.

I don't know how'd you'd ever recognise an old urupā, but I'm sure I found it. The kahikatea trees were there right where the stories said they would be, but far apart across the little stream. For some reason, I expected to see a fence or wire strung across some pigtails, but there wasn't any. On one side of the aukati was me and the stream, on the other side of the aukati was just the stream. Just like you boys want to, I stepped over the line.

Nothing happened at first, but it was dark—dark enough for me to think I'd better be getting home. I took maybe five steps more and stopped. Just around a small bend, I could see a branch planted in the bank. It looked identical to the one I held in my hand, right down to the hatchet marks. I took one more step towards it and that was enough for me to see what was in the water.

Son, I'm not going to tell you what I saw. I've never told anyone what I saw. All I'm going to say is that I've never seen a deeper trench of water and that Chris had not gone back to Auckland.

Don't go with them, my son. I'm telling you, you do not want to cross that line.

CARIN SMEATON

Why She Quit Queen at Night

cos anywhere's safer than sleepin shallow on queen street in deep night never deep enuf tho to hide her from dem young ones wit their shark skin suits and radar brows made for catchin jumpy heart-beats and hers would let out an irregular vibration like a wounded echo in a sinkhole leadin em di-rect to her & lee (they been together 2 years since she were kickt outta home out west and she ain't never been back) and it'd take jus one of dem young ones to land her one in the jaw smash her teeth in top to bottom leavin a hole too big to whistle thru too small to cry over but even then she still is pretty as a petal for an old gal in her twenties lee says and she'd laugh and show him her pretty bloody gums and go wit a shrug n short memory to the hospital where they'd fix her up good n proper cos they already knows her from last time the day she lay dazed on the concrete next to lee wit her ear to the pavement knowin she could hear the water of the waihorotiu flowin to swellin under the sewer below made 4 disappearin in a direction only she could calculate wit her inbuilt compass her north star hearin it movin not stoppin magnetic all the way and as long as it never stood still never stopped stagnant she knew it would get to where it were goin cos she could hear it go torrential and it sounded alive   and she understood that

ERIK KENNEDY

Amores

It's hard to love someone for who they are, so we dress up for weddings.
The wave withdraws from around your feet, and your toes cause the biggest eddies.

The scientific consensus is: *no screens in bed*.
This new bamboo pillow lets me forget that I have a head.

Moving in with someone marks a 'strange new stage of life'.
I used to wait until the fruits were ripe to pick them off the greengage.

Those tree branches shaped like lovers' swings cup the buttocks just right.
They describe a parabola that goes, returningly, from night to erotic night.

When they melt down the love locks from the Pont des Arts, they can build a tank.
But do I look like the sort of guy who'd accept a ride from a stranger in a tank?! No thanks.

Trying to control who the control freak is in a two-control-freak relationship
is a form of democratic dictatorship (according to an unofficial leak).

Oh, why does the sun, that meddling twonk, rise before our alarm, my darling?
I remember when dawn was a thing a private security firm was supposed to be guarding.

An illicit brothel has opened in England Street, and it's 'as busy as McDonald's'.
It's an amusingly small bottleneck through which the desires are funnelled.

Take the years you've spent alone and multiply them by five. That's your real
 age.
Turquoise's complementary colour is beige, so forget it! Do the nursery in
 Spanish white.

Soviet lander *Luna 18* lies in a heap forever at the edge of the Sea of Fertility.
Now that's what I call emotion recollected in tranquillity.

I think it was Lucretius who said that falling in love is like having drunk three
 bottles of wine the night before,
and that love is actually all we can eat or drink, and that's what makes us
 omnivores.

PETER PERYER

PHOTOGRAPHS

1. *Blood Veil, 2015, 200 x 300 mm. Digital print.*
2. *Gibbston, Central Otago, 2008, 200 x 300 mm. Digital print.*
3. *Pillars, 2015, 200 x 300 mm. Digital print.*
4. *Lanterns, 2010, 200 x 300 mm. Digital print.*
5. *Calla Lilies, 2012, 200 x 300 mm. Digital print.*
6. *Coral Reef, 2013, 200 x 300 mm. Digital print.*
7. *Umbrellas, Fiji, 2013, 200 x 300 mm. Digital print.*
8. *Veil, 2012, 200 x 300 mm. Digital print.*

Peter Peryer has always had a camera close at hand. First it was a two and a quarter inch square reflex that he held at waist height and looked down into to see what image he was taking. Then it was 35 mm cameras that he held up to his eye. Now it's an iPhone with its own distinctive gestures ... But in all the years we've known him we've only ever seen Peter take three or four photographs that have ended up as what he calls 'keepers'.
—Jim and Mary Barr, Peter Peryer: A careful eye (Dowse Art Gallery catalogue, 2014)

I can't help it—I keep taking photographs that remind me of photographs that I have taken before, although always hopeful that the most recent will, in flavour and tone at least, add something to its predecessor.
—Peter Peryer

LEILANI TAMU

Researching Ali`i

I searched for you in boxes
    the archivist muttered *poison*

I searched for you in texts
    the librarian whispered *incest*

I searched for you in images
    the cashier demanded *money*

I found you in mele
    the people chant *aloha*

ALLISON LI

The Not Quite Full Moon

You make a lousy lover, but you are
    a million bucks
in suits that look like designers
only make for you
Cigarette ash blows out the window
embers glow and scatter
    into the wind

Sinking into the back seat
I draw a lungful of second-hand
    smoke, exhale
what transpired between us
It was one scorching summer
where dreams venture for longer than
    they are sustained

The congregation starts, farewell
    fair-weather friend
for the one on your arm
in ribbon and lace
The keeper of your heart
    is not me
and can never be

Exchanging small-talk
over broken china, tears stain
lip print pressed
    to handkerchief
my world undoes at the seam

I can't want you any more
    but I do

I scrub ache away in the basin
your amulet slips from my neck
    down the drain
the last remnants of you disappear
How can an eternal summer fade
surely there is a season to all things
    save for love

Residues of you travel
through the recess of my mind
where you shall reside for as long
    as you want
I haven't a reason to believe
    you are gone
and I don't believe you

RATA GORDON

A Baby

I want to make a baby out of one peach and one prickle.
I want to use the kitchen sponge, sticky rice and a rubber band.
I want to use the coffee grinder.

I want to make a baby out of concrete and a jackhammer.
I want to use the oil on the driveway.
I want to use rainwater, a cigarette butt and a milk bottle.

I want to make a baby out of wet sand and a nappy.
I want to use micro-plastics and plasma.
I want to use cockles and cable-ties and chip packets and pipis.

I want the baby to wake up and cry out.
I want the baby to cry out.
I want to make a baby.

VICTORIA BROOME

And we have all been each other's mothers over countless lifetimes

Mum, Mum,
I was your mum once, we shared a
heartbeat and a pulse and we slipped
through a tear in the cosmos.
I am calling, always calling,
my voice is orbiting:
it is a little satellite as aeons pass.
You go whirling by in your pink nylon dressing gown
back in time, forward in time,
until you are tucked up again and uterine.

SIOBHAN HARVEY

The Pocket Atlas of Personal Property

A moon filter is a physical thing,
like the Sea of Serenity and Pacific Plate.
It possesses the momentum of the tide
retreating in the estuary, ancient middens
revealed, the buzzing of displaced bees
and electric heat of fruit on branch waiting
to fall. Barlow lens, dew shield, telescope,
flashlight: here are more galactic treasures.
They compose a story, a star map of
Spaceboy's most precious things.

Lined upon window ledge, they create
such synchronicity as holds Rutherford
and Bohr, posters fixed to wall, in place.
And the view beyond the open window
where the Sun has swallowed properties,
a series of state houses, their long corridors, landings,
starflowers decorating wallpaper, and gardens
grounded by trampolines and tree houses.

Each night while physicists watch over
astronomical objects which watch over
a landscape deteriorating into a black hole,
Spaceboy considers the relativity and chaos
of his neighbourhood, the compact mass
of land emptied of homes, their gravity still
palpable. When he closes his eyes, sleep is
a series of star-instruments, dreams navigating
the coordinates of turmoil and imminent collapse.

Spaceboy and the White Hole

In stargazing, Spaceboy is a night sky,
in his presence the drama of how we live
in two dimensions unfolds, the electricity of
the present fused to the power of the past.

Sculptor, Phoenix ... he whispers. Fierce as
furnace, his eyes scan his family close by
settled warmly around an outside heater.
He sees their faces are faint reflections
of how he came to be. Turning away,

he pictures matter barely visible, the light
of white holes as they transmit their secret
messages, sharp elegies, about letting go.

RUTH ARNISON

The Visit

Even from the road her house gave us the creeps.
Pale, communion wafer thin, and disapproving,
its severe windows three-quarter blinded.

In the front room, where Aunt Bess hooked rugs,
six straight-backed feet-can't-reach-the-ground chairs
sat in front of the ill-fed too-lethargic-to-crackle fire.

Her clock tocked loudly, teasing us with its long minutes.
Dispatched to the kitchen *to help* we plated mouldy
fruitcake and time-softened biscuits.

We quivered holding in our nervous laughter, avoiding
eye contact while passing our parents these offerings.
We'd left out hunger in the kitchen.

We hung on, crossed legs, hung on, too scared to sit
over the long-drop's bottomless hole. As if she knew,
she pointed to the chamber pot lurking in the pantry.

We raced outside, threw ourselves into the long grass
by the gooseberry bushes, whooping and wheezing
with relief.

Fifty years on, the house and long-drop have gone.
The nearby estuary gurgles with contentment.

SAM KEENAN

Every Family

Every family has this photograph:
paddling pool with Dad and kid.
Nothing's as perfect as a paper past:

the plastic fish, the perpetual laugh,
Mum out of shot with cake candles lit.
Every family has this photograph,

unless, of course, it's been torn in half
the day your mother finally quit,
saw her exit and fumbled past.

Memory is not so colourfast.
No one frames the cry, *You little shit!*
but every family has this photograph,

even the ones who can't be arsed,
who, given the choice, would give kids a miss.
It pays to reinvent the past,

to cut it into squares and cover it with glass,
to prune the unwanted bit by bit,
so that every family has this photograph,
because nothing's as perfect as a paper past.

JILLIAN SULLIVAN

Some Things About My Life

Growing up
On the day of the nativity reading, my mother put a lamb roast in the oven. She took off her apron and put on her white gloves.

In the early days of church, I sat next to my father in the pew through interminable sermons and stodgy songs. *O God, our help in ages past* ... When I fidgeted too much he'd pass me an envelope and pen from his pocket and I'd sit and draw. It looked like scribble to anyone else. To me it was the floor plan of the church, seen from above, complete with new steeple, a large organ, and rows filled with people in their Sunday best.

The day of the readings I was eight. My mother was the pianist. She always played the piano in church, even when she didn't want to, and shouted in our kitchen she wasn't going *one more time*; she was tired, no one appreciated the hours she spent in practice, how she gave up every Wednesday night for choir and still had to clean the church in the roster on Thursdays.

Mum sat at the keys and when I stepped out by the altar to read my nativity lines I looked across at her. She raised her fingers with that quietness she got when she was over the shouting and had finally accepted her lot. She nodded at me, then played the first few lines of 'Silent Night'.

'And there were in the same country shepherds abiding in the field, keeping watch over their flock by night. And, lo, the angel of the Lord came upon them, and the glory of the Lord shone round about them: and they were sore afraid.'

In the front row, if I'd drawn an updated floor plan of the church from above, I would have seen how Mrs Miller, dressed in a white lace blouse and blue skirt, was positioned: slightly forward and across from my father, who was in the sixth row with my sister.

'And the angel said unto them, Fear not ...' Here I paused the way Mum had coached me, to let those words sink in. Only I forgot to take a breath. '... For unto you is born this day in the city of David a Saviour ...'

'Thank you. And may the Blessed Jesus, forever in our midst, watch over us and protect us all,' said Reverend Kirk. 'Amen.'

My reading happened to be the only verses of the Bible I memorised, that being our absolutely last day ever in church, on account of Mrs Miller and the affair she was having with my father. My mother realised this as she played the last chords of 'Love Divine, All Loves Excelling'. She looked up uncharacteristically from her music and caught the look between my father and the side of Mrs Miller's face. My sister and I learnt this later.

The words of Luke Chapter 2 verses 8–14 did me great service for the next seven years. I recited them to my pony Rosie whenever we faced imminent death. Rosie was my loyal companion now our family was ruined. She didn't like trucks, barking dogs that ran out driveways, ducks that flapped unexpectedly from ditches, or pieces of paper blown about on the verge. Mostly she was terrified of sheep trucks. If we were on a narrow road and I heard one of those sheep trucks coming, I'd start to pray.

Not 'Blessed Jesus, please help us.' I'd already worked out that prayer wasn't going to save our family. I'd discovered the power of Luke Chapter 2 when I was ten and Rosie and I were in our third face-off with a sheep truck.

'There were in the same country shepherds abiding in the field ...' I'd blurted out, and my faith in the power of those words had transmitted itself to Rosie. She stood by the side of the road, trembling, and let the truck pass, instead of rearing up, running backwards and sideways and doing her best to throw us both under the wheels.

Dad didn't know Mum had seen him look at Mrs Miller. And we didn't know about the rumours Mum had heard. We walked home from church that day and all I thought about was the roast lamb to come, and my favourite roast potatoes, once Dad got home with the shopping.

He put the bag on the kitchen table. I fossicked in the cutlery drawer for the matching forks and knives, and my mother took the potatoes and stood there for a moment.

'I saw you,' she said to him. I looked up from the drawer. This was almost her shouting-at-the-piano voice. The voice that trembled before the onslaught.

'You dirty skunk!' The first potato missed my father and smashed the kitchen clock.

Potato after potato. She didn't care where they went. A few hit Dad hard on the side of the head. My little sister Bella started to scream. I pulled her down onto the floor and squeezed her. The clock fell off the wall. Dad slammed the door. The potatoes went on banging against it, and my sister and I yelling. The cacophony was enough to set a horse's hair on end.

'In church!' Mum screamed. 'In *church!*' Another potato hit the door. I guessed we wouldn't be having roast potatoes. Or solace from any kind of food.

The next Sunday I got up and dressed in my orange check dress that Mum liked and I abhorred. I put on white socks and my black shoes and dressed Bella, who was four, in the exact same outfit, without being asked. In the kitchen Mum was in her dressing gown and the oven was cold. 'That is the last time we set foot in that church,' my mother said. 'The last time *ever*. In front of the whole congregation! Probably everybody knew.'

'Are you going to throw potatoes again?' asked Bella.

Our mother just looked out the window.

'Are you going to play the piano again?' Bella asked. I didn't ask anything because I was not my mother's favourite child.

'Of course I am,' my mother said. 'Why would you stop doing the one thing you believe in? Now go outside and play.'

The fact that it was raining had escaped her. I took Bella up to my room and let her play with my walkie-talkie doll, Angela, the doll Bella had ruined when she was two. She'd wrecked Angela's long, shiny hair so completely I'd hacked the whole lot off. Now Angela was only used as Jesus in the school play at Christmas and for bribing Bella on occasions such as this.

I had a taste like ashes in my mouth. Bella hummed and called Angela 'that slut Mrs Miller' as she tucked her into her bed. I sat on my bed and looked out the window at the rain.

What did I believe in? Only my pony, even if she was determined to do us both in. And the need for shelter.

Our father had moved out. I thought about this for a while—practical considerations, like what to say to my best friend Susan when she asked where he'd gone. Bella hummed. My mother played loudly on the piano in the sitting room.

I stopped thinking about my fatherless state and thought about Rosie, who, apart from her habit of terrifying me, also had a disfiguring skin condition. Not only did she not win prizes in any show, but in winter her beautiful brown hair fell out in clumps. It was summer now and she was shiny, but the thought of winter, and the lumps under her skin coming back, and the skin-caked slices of hair that came away under my fingers when I patted her made me cry.

Bella climbed up on my bed. She sucked beside me for a while, then took her thumb out of her mouth.

'We hate her, don't we?' she said.

Our letter of reference called my husband and me hard workers, our children happy and well looked after. We got the job. He went to work on the chicken farm, where the owner called him Boy, or Billy Boy if it was a good day. The perk, of course, was eggs—we got all the cracked ones.

I grew zucchinis in the moist soil by the creek, down by the plum tree. We ate zucchini fritters and plum pie and variations on this (stewed plums, zucchini pie). There was always enough of everything that grew down by the creek.

But not of money. So as well as eggs, my husband brought home from work his hot frustration, his scarred hands, his tired feet. And all the pies in the world could not cover the rift that gaped between us.

'Perhaps I'll become an architect,' I said. I wasn't joking.

Almost better than a job that gives life meaning is the job where you are appreciated. How do you get appreciated? If you take your thwarted power home, is it any use—the silence that fear brings?

We ate a lot of omelettes and devilled eggs, but never chicken, because I don't believe in cages. Chicken could have solved a lot of problems, but there are lines you have to draw. If I couldn't keep back the names I was called, I could at least spurn those dimpled carcases and make another pie.

We'd got married when we were eighteen. My mother said I should learn to live in the bed I had made, so I didn't tell her anything.

Our Vauxhall Viva died one hot Thursday afternoon when I was miles from home. In the back seat our children: Georgia, seven; Lucy, four; Frederick, eight months. The brakes weren't that great either.

The first car that came along was the neighbour who grew tomatoes in glasshouses beside the chicken farm. I think he grew the tomatoes in chicken shit. They were good tomatoes but he would talk to us like we were the *workers*: people who would just move on and weren't part of the community. His good samaritanness prevailed, though, when he saw me standing on the side of the road looking under the bonnet in case there were instructions.

'Are you out of petrol?' he asked me.

'No, but I might have been low on oil.'

He looked at the temperature gauge and tried the key in the ignition. He went back to his boot for a tow rope.

'I'll tow you to the top of McWaynes Hill and you're on your own from there, okay? I don't want this car coming down behind me on that slope.'

'Is that safe?'

'Nothing's safe. This road isn't safe. Those chickens you eat probably aren't safe.'

'I don't eat the chickens. I eat your tomatoes.'

At the brow of the hill he disconnected our cars.

'I'll pick you up again at the bottom.' His arm waved out and he was down around the corner.

I looked over at the back seat. 'You girls buckled in still?'

The two girls nodded back at me. Okay, brake off. The car slowly rumbled, gathered speed.

My father came from a line of Rechabites, an order founded in the 1840s committed to complete abstinence from alcohol. No one drank in our house. No one mentioned alcohol. No one brought it into the house. We didn't even know people who drank.

The day my mother was to go on television, my father came home at lunchtime and caught her celebrating with a bottle of champagne.

Wine! A green glass bottle with a fluid inside so dangerous it had the power to destroy our family. He threw the bottle out the window and punched my mother in the head. She had her lipstick on and her hair already done for the interview. (My mother had written a piece of music for the piano so stunningly beautiful she'd won a national award.)

Bella and I set to screaming. Our mother said, 'Go up to your bedroom and stay there.' Instead Bella flung herself on Mum's feet, as if that would help the situation. I didn't know anything better to do than to cry, and to stand next to Dad, where my allegiance generally lay, except for the punch. His fists at his side were a strange colour of white.

McWaynes Hill is not the steepest hill in the country but you wouldn't want to trot down it if you were riding. The Vauxhall gathered speed until it was shaking, and my fists on the wheel that same bloodless colour *trying to keep a hold of the situation.*

How fast were we going? We flung around the corner, and there was a police car coming up the other side. He had to go all the way to the top but sure enough he came back after us.

The hill flattened out in the same abrupt manner the slope started. The car swooped soundlessly along the road, just the noise of the tyres on the tarseal. No engine. No baby crying or girls squabbling. All of us probably bug-eyed with fright.

The car slowed to a trundle and I pulled off on the side of the road and stopped just before the cop got to us. Because sometimes there is a God.

My mother's piece of music was called 'Joy'. If you asked me now to play it, or even hum it, the most I could manage would be the first few bars. It was never recorded because after the TV interview someone at the recording studio stole my mother's only manuscript. We heard it got performed in Australia. Mum could still play it—she remembers everything she ever learnt on the piano right back to when she was six years old—but she won't. And she never wrote another song.

When she went on TV she had her hair fixed up and lipstick back on and she smiled so much she looked happy. And a lot later on she was. A lot later than the punch. A bit later than Mrs Miller and the potatoes.

The cop walked around the car without speaking to me. He checked the rego and the warrant. He checked the tyres. He motioned for me to wind down the window.

'You kids all right?' he asked them.

'Do you know I am a cat?' said Lucy. He looked at her a bit longer and went once more around the car checking the tyres again.

'Don't say stuff like that, Lucy,' said Georgia. 'Especially not to policemen.'

'But I am.' Her precious child-face serious in the rear-vision mirror.

'Is Freddie asleep?' I asked them.

Georgia leant over to peer in the car seat.

'He's blowing bubbles.'

The cop asked for my driving licence and I passed it to him.

'You weren't speeding, but you didn't look like you were comfortable coming down that hill.'

'I pull faces sometimes,' I said.

He passed me back my licence and drove off. There was no sign of the tomato man. I did one of those big sighs like my mother does sometimes. Could I push the car home? I slumped over the steering wheel. Perhaps we would just stay the night there, since the car wasn't going to do anything of its own accord.

Or I could get out and hitch with the three of them.

'You are not a cat,' said Georgia. 'And when you go to school you can't say stuff like that or you're not my sister.'

'Mum. When do I go to school?'

'Not for another year. Not till it's been winter again and back to summer.' How sane and logical I was, curled over the wheel.

'Then I won't, Georgie. After that.'

Right before Freddie started to cry, wanting a feed, the tomato grower's ute came back for us. But it was our own man driving. I did have a knight in shining armour after all.

In all my life I've never met another horse whose hair fell out in winter. I had a pony with a skin condition, and when I was a teenager I had acne. No one else in my family got acne. It was just me and Rosie, as if we ate something.

Now I lived in the countryside on a chicken farm with my family, miles from town and the library and the source of any other food apart from eggs, tomatoes, plums and zucchinis. There were five of us, and now no car. How were we going to get to a shop?

Late afternoon my husband came down to the stream with me, Freddie in the backpack. We sat by the loamy soil to talk about the car situation. I raked my fingers back and forward in the warmth of dirt. Back and forward. I was the one who didn't check the oil that morning.

My dad used to recite poetry he'd learnt at high school fifty years earlier. At my high school we studied the language of advertising. I learnt how to tell the truths or untruths behind language. Nothing on how to get by, though.

Dad: 'The fears of what may come to pass/ I cast them all away/ Among the clover-scented grass/ among the new mown hay ...'

I'd just mown the grass down there, with the last of the petrol from the container in the car boot. Sweet, slightly fermenting clover. I laid my back down into it.

'I want my life to mean something,' I said up to the sky. I lay there a bit longer. No one said anything. Not even Freddie. When I sat up Harry was weeding creeping mellow from around the zucchini plants.

'I could go back to school,' I said.

I watched his fingers. For some reason the chicken shit burned his skin, even when he wore gloves. Perhaps it was just the smell of it. When I looked at the back of his hands, rashed for the love of us, I forgave him everything. I wanted to reach out and touch him. I wanted to say ...

Once, before Rosie and I were kicked out of pony club (after Rosie kicked the instructor), our club had travelled to the fields of the national One Day Event. We cantered our inconspicuous mounts along the trail those big-hearted warm-bloods galloped. We looked up at the jumps as we rode past: full wire fences with tyres on top, ditches forty feet wide (or so it seemed.) At the top of a cliff, Miss Hutchinson told us how the horses and riders went over the top, down a trail so steep the horses had to sit on their rumps and slide.

When she turned and rode away, the other kids followed her, but I rode Rosie up to the edge of the cliff. I wanted to see. Rosie took a step closer. I peered down that rump-slick track.

She took another step. Oh, how she went anywhere my heart wanted. I didn't want the cliff, but she went anyway. There was a moment when I could have jumped off. I leaned back in the saddle instead, like cowboys do, faced with a grand canyon in front and Indians behind.

'And there were in the same country shepherds abiding in the field …' I chanted, before Rosie was on her rump, her front feet splayed, sliding. It was all I could do to stay on her back and stay balanced so I didn't pitch her, face over tail, to the stream below. Never mind the Bible.

'What do you think?' I asked my husband.

'About what?' He kept weeding, and Freddie, who was still asleep in the backpack, followed the tugging action of Harry's hands with a jiggle of his warm, bare feet.

'About going to university.'

'I'm not going back to university. What are you talking about?'

'I mean me, Harry. I could be an architect. And one day I'll be able to buy us a car.'

'We need one now,' he said. 'How are you going to get food?' He looked across the fifteen zucchini plants, still in full production. 'And please don't plant this many again.'

'I know. Even I'm sick of them.' I said. I lay back down. Freddie was asleep and Georgia and Lucy were in the sandpit far behind me. I lay in the clover-scented grass and breathed deeply.

Harry wouldn't go to university, or study anything that would take us away from the chicken farm, I knew that. And it was all right. I knew I had a stronger spirit; I knew what I loved: the kids first, and then who I was, and then him. I knew it wasn't love like in the movies, but I loved him enough. And I loved my life more—that I had that chance, that I could pass those exams.

And I have what I carry inside me: that Rosie went over the cliff and I went with her. Not everyone has that; or potatoes in their past; or their mother, punched, on TV; or Bach and Chopin early morning, late at night. Or even the way to grow zucchinis by the stream, under the plum tree and a hazel sky.

JOHANNA EMENEY

Prayer

On the seventh day
when you texted to say
that your sister was no better,
that still sepsis raged
against the trial and error
of the doctors' best guesses,

it broke my heart
(this was the rip and ache
behind the top left ribs
I felt for your sake)
when you explained
that your prayers

must not have been enough
to wake her from the coma
the specialist had induced
and now could not undo
with a slow barbiturate taper, nor
later, with a risky adrenaline shot.

Now, I've taken responsibility
for many things in my life,
but they were far smaller,
like a forbidden water fight;
a till, while the shopkeeper
took a short break;

a dog that skated on a frozen lake
when I let him off-leash,
and children who stayed up
much too late on my watch—
but I have never held myself to blame
for medicine's hit-and-miss treatments,

nor for the body's snap decisions, its hairline
fractures, its bad cancer grades. If I had,
I'd be scab-kneed and white-knuckled to this day,
uttering prayers for a mother to uncrumple,
stand and walk backwards, away
from her own wreckage.

HEATHER MCQUILLAN

In which I defend our father's right to solitude

our father has a fine tooth way
of finding vulnerabilities
on the outward flanks
    the wolf is always at his door

our father was a sent-away boy
folded neatly in the crossfire of war
a small suitcase on a train
a paper label on string
a stranger in a strange land
    he cannot breathe in this place

our father was a run-away boy
soot-dripped standing
on bomb-scorched steps of a no-more-home
    I see the shadow slip into his pores

our father pedalled hard into head winds
whenever the norwest blew, he bent,
a wrongness occupied his head
and his dreams, displaced, fled far away.
    we learned empathy—and silence—on those days

to combat his fears our father donned a stage presence,
an armour, and a fine, strong voice.
I'd fled from home before sharp wounds
and the shadowy dog finally shot our father down.
      I never heard him sing again

our father's life is an enfilade—or enfilaade
he would need to know that one way was right—
uncertainties shudder him to the core

he will not leave the house now
cannot breathe outside
not since
our mother died

DOC DRUMHELLER

My Father's Fingers

Days after my father died I felt a sense
of urgency to take care of his hot-house.

It was early spring and his tomatoes
were already five feet tall and rising.

Small green fruit poked out of yellow flowers
protruding like an outie belly button.

His cucumber vines began to climb
his banana peppers were small but sturdy.

Then came the frosts that spread like cancer
then came the aphids acting like assassins.

But there will be no sprays on his tomatoes
no poisons on his peppers and cucumbers.

I washed each leaf by hand as I couldn't bear
to lose the final things his fingers touched.

WES LEE

Fire-walker

One of those nights on repeat that clouded
my teenage. I thought dads were all that way,
rolling unfeeling over stones—no gravel
or hot coals could burn enough, immune,

I know now you drank to be a fire-walker,
a circus performer, to dull all nerves, to fly
for a few hours with your words
and your audience of men somewhere else.

The eyes of women you would roll home to,
towering above as you laughed and obviously
thought you were clever. We held our feet back,
stayed our hands from your neck to wring you

like the preposterous turkey escaping the pot.
And years later, in a draughty hall,
a man is led in and shook to the front; trembled
at the microphone to release the words

that work like a baptism.

KOENRAAD KUIPER

From *Benedictine Sonnets*

II.
Mother always knitted particularly socks.
Knitting socks is a fine skill under the lamplight.
You knit with double-pointed short needles
maybe size 7 and a tough worsted wool.

Knitting socks is best done in the evening.
It is soothing. The needles click and the fire burns.
The clicking is regular and occasionally the fire crackles,
the embers glow and a sock slowly comes to exist.

First the leg section, a tube with a cuff,
then the heel flap and two triangular sections on each side,
around the corner and into the foot section

another tube ending at the toe with a single thread hanging
like a black hair on a witch's nose.
I still have three pairs. They have outlived their maker.

CAOIMHE MCKEOGH

Time Trails

At 1am, Aunt Lily was kneeling on the floor of her kitchen pretending to be an atheist boy who had just seen my boobs for the first time and was thanking God for their existence. (This was how she shut me up when I complained that I was too fat to ever get a boyfriend.) By 2am things had become more serious, and we were designing our own theory of time.

We decided that every lifetime trails behind its user like a string, but winds up into tight spirals for the days, weeks, months, years when things are pretty much the same. So when we look back, interesting things are distinct memories, but routines are only represented as one generalised version of the many times they were carried through. Little changes can make new spirals, though—'the months of high school when my hair was blue' stand distinct from the leftover years of red. We decided that if you wanted to have a longer life, you just had to change things more often.

That was Portland, Oregon, in a flat near the road lined with food carts. In my American year I was too shy to take photographs, so I can't remember the colour of the walls, or whether she'd been kneeling on carpet or wood. But I didn't forget to change.

In Manchester I wore jeans and woollen jumpers, cuddled a class of five-year-olds from 9 to 3 on weekdays, and smiled every time someone said, 'I can't believe you're only eighteen!'

In Toulouse I dressed all in black with my jeans tucked into men's boots and tried not to talk to anyone. I stayed up until every sunrise watching English TV shows, and dropped by the 24-hour supermarket at 5am to stare at the middle-aged cashier with the retainer on his teeth, wondering whether he'd start a conversation.

In Germany I was a capable backpacker who led lost tourists to ATMs and bus stops, knew how to sleep well on an overnight train, said, 'No, I haven't been here long at all, but you get used to it quickly, you'll see—I already catch myself saying, "home"!'

But then the bank account was empty and the travelling was over and it was time to go to university. All the lives I'd lived since high school were stretched out behind me inside two years, but it takes three to do a bachelor of arts.

I became a person who said, 'It only feels like yesterday ...'

All the times I walked through Aro Park overlaid into a single image of pigeons and sun-faded bunting, apart from the one day that somebody had cut off their dreadlocks and laid them down the middle of the path. They seemed shockingly severed, like pig trotters, and made their own tiny spiral of string in my memory. Months of mornings struggling up Devon Street and afternoons coming heavily back down have conflated, but I remember the day I walked home so fast that my knees almost couldn't keep up with me. I'd left a warm, solid body in my bed that morning and was hoping that time had paused in my absence, so I could slide back in beside him, smell garlic and beer and last night on his skin.

And there he was. He'd pushed the duvet onto the floor where it somehow coiled between the three sweaty cans of Bavaria that had been abandoned there last night, all still upright. His head was under the pillow, his hands on top of it, pale pink briefs tucked in on one side so a single rounded buttock peeked out. He didn't move at all when I closed the door a little too hard—for at least half a second I wondered whether he was dead.

But then he emerged, ear first, from under the pillow and said, 'What happened? Where's your class? I dreamed you were a book with teeth!' and a new spiral began, where there was someone holding my hand when I walked down the path in Aro Park, and someone who disappeared for days motorbiking around the country and not replying to texts, while I watched YouTube videos of traffic accidents, read stories about the lives of people who've sustained brain damage, pretended not to be staring at my phone out the corner of my eye, and wondered how it was possible for time to go so very slowly.

This was the first spiral of my life where sleep didn't feel too important. After years of travelling with eye covers and ear plugs, my teenage screaming at siblings who played music too loudly on a Saturday morning, a life of melatonin tablets and lavender oil baths ... now I turned my phone onto its loudest setting when I went to bed, so that if Alex texted me at 4am saying, 'Hey, what are you up to?' I could reply, 'Not much. You?' I would rather lie for hours with his sweaty forearm on my face, listening to his breath whistle slightly in and out, than have a good eight hours alone to prepare me for the day to come. In the morning he'd tell me, 'I dreamed you were a dancer and I came to your show. I was so scared you'd mess up, but you didn't.' 'I dreamed you had a cat that only had three legs. All the bits of its face were in the wrong places, but you loved it, you still thought it was beautiful.' 'I dreamed we went for a walk and wore traffic cones for hats, but that wasn't a weird thing to do, and they weren't heavy.'

When he lost his job and sold his bike, it became every day that I would come home from my classes and find him still in bed, but now he was turned towards the wall and his eyes were usually open. Now time that was slow was the worst sort of time. Sitting together on the couch, me suggesting activities and him rejecting each one, watching too many episodes of too many shows, wanting the laptop clock to get a move on so it would be bedtime and we'd have something we had to do.

He went to a job interview. He couldn't tell me whether it had gone well, but after the interview he'd gone through the wrong door looking for a bathroom, and ended up in a stationery cupboard off a room where a meeting was beginning. When he heard people coming, he for some reason closed the door on himself. He was too embarrassed to come out, so he stayed for almost two hours listening to three men and one woman discussing the business's finances. He invented life stories for each of them based on their voices, while becoming more and more desperate to pee. He told me it had been tranquil and anxious at the same time, and I should try it some day: they'd been the slowest two hours of his life. 'Maybe if you lived in a cupboard, you'd live forever.'

  I didn't invite my parents to my graduation. I didn't want them to spend money and time coming all the way down to Wellington, and I didn't want to force them to be in the same room and be polite to each other. But that night, after Alex went to bed, I called them both to fill them in about my life, and then I called Aunt Lily for the first time in years, suddenly shy.

'I got my BA today!'

'Well done, darling.'

'Nah, it was easy. The only question was whether I'd stick it out for so long, but I did …'

'Well, I've been hearing occasional stories about a boyfriend—from your dad?'

'Yeah, Alex, that's a thing. I really love him.'

'Oh god, it's terrifying isn't it? I remember falling in love with your uncle.'

'Yeah?'

'Oh babe, I was never going to fall in love! That leads to getting married and having children and I didn't want any of those things …'

'What were you planning to do?'

'I had no plans, really … travel, maybe … I have travelled, I guess.'

'You live in America now!'

'Yeah. I think I just fancied myself being a little more bohemian than this.'

'Do you remember the night we came up with that thing about time being a string?'

'Oh god, just about! Have you been making your life longer by filling it with memories?'

'Sort of. But I've been in the same place for three years …'

'Well, you're done now! If you'd like, you can come and live with us for a while … Marilyn from next door runs a childcare centre and I know you have experience with kids—we could sort something out.'

'I think Alex is going back to uni. He can't get a job and he's been feeling a bit useless, but he might try again with getting a degree.'

'And you?'

'I might just go back too. Do Honours or something …'

'So you're sticking close.'

'Sometimes I think about leaving him, but then I think about waking up in the morning and not having him tell me about his latest weird dream, or lying in bed at night without being able to whisper to him about my day, waking up in a muddle after a nightmare and there's only my arms and legs, not his …'

'Do you have lots in common?'

'All the bits that matter.'

'I still love your uncle, twenty years later.'

'Are the whole twenty years one big ball of string?'

'Of course not. Well, I dunno … I think time goes faster as you get older; there's not much anyone can do about that. But I usually don't regret marrying him.'

'Yeah?'

'There are days, but I'm so glad I have him. The boys ... I dunno ... I love the boys to death. Now there's nothing I'd do to change them, but having kids is a lifetime commitment; sometimes I wonder how I'd have been without them.'

'Are they your main life thing?'

'I guess so ... my two biggest achievements. I'm happy.'

'Okay. I'll think about your offer to come and stay.'

'Yes, do!'

'But I have a student loan, and no money for a plane ticket. It's a lot harder to pack up and leave than it used to be.'

'Ha, you're such an adult! Isn't it glorious? Well, call again sometime, babe.'

'Yeah, okay. Thank you.'

I went into the bathroom with a pair of scissors and tried to cut off my two girlish plaits, but it was a lot harder than I'd expected. I did enough damage to be sure I'd have to go to the hairdresser's and get it cut short, though, which I'd been wondering about doing for months.

Then I left a note for Alex saying, 'Gone for a walk!' and set off across town and up Mount Vic to look out across the tiny, sparkling city and decide whether or not to stay for another spiral ...

MADELINE REID

Sugar Town

The motor lodge was doing filtered coffee, 2 for 1, all day long. All the gumbooted bogans piled in, demanding mugs with ten-cent pieces. Only a few of the scripted regulars showed up, placing orders for vine-ripe tomatoes and Vogel's. The crowd was vastly different from the usual clientele. The barkeep wandered around with sweat pouring out of his ears, coughing tersely through drawn lips as the spittle washed onto his apron and he waited for the coffee to bulk and foam and percolate in its beaker.

He dropped a bit of aspirin in his coffee, clearing the baccarat table with a free hand.

'Dana,' he shouted, clutching furiously at the end of the receiver, 'get your arse in here. We're swarmed. Tom, Jerry and truckies bloody everywhere! Muttons dressed in lamb, Dana. Muttons dressed in *lamb*.'

Dana had spent the morning on a spontaneous climb up Mt Tamahunga. As the pinkie dawn rose, she grew giddy and drunk, swinging her legs over the crown and downing skulls of Bacardi through a torn plastic Shell bag.

'Robert Johnson sold his soul to the devil,' she said to Brett. 'On the crossroads, in the middle of the goddamn night.'

'I dunno,' said Brett. 'I heard he was poisoned. That's how he died. The devil taught him the blues.'

'Nobody's born evil,' she said, like it was a fact. 'Nobody, I reckon.'

The sun was rising above the gulf, drawing a coppered ring of light over the ranges. When they looked hard enough all the hidden details of the landscape were made available to them: the winched-out mudslides cratered in the mountainside; the haze of gold paint rounding trees, mushrooming out of the ground in ovals and beckoning to the sky like tiny piebald owls.

'Did I hear a phone before?' Brett said.

'It's probably mine,' she said. She tugged her zipper, playing with the tag. 'Don't worry about it. It's only work.'

'Bastards. Didn't you just come from there?'

'From an all-night shift, yeah. It's no big deal though,' she said, emphasising the 'no' so he would know that it was, in fact, *a very big deal*. 'I promised myself I wouldn't go in today. It's my only day off.'

'Vince will be here soon.'

She scowled. 'Vince. Vince is coming with us today.'

'That's right.'

A pause.

'I thought you knew I hate Vince.'

'I do,' he said. 'Really, I do know that. But he knows all the best contacts in town—he got me this liquor—I don't have to rely on my brother now.'

Dana swallowed this fact and recoiled at once, feeling hopeless and defeated and swallowed. The only way they ever got their drink was through his brother, who dished it out behind the Lifeguard shack on the dunes at Omaha, slipping in some candy bars for the currency, like a mild privilege. 'Here you go, kids. Keep it eighteen.'

'Come on,' he said, losing control of his laughter and himself, with another swig. 'He's not that bad.'

His laugh was stiff and unfunny. It settled over the atmosphere like insipid gas settling into the lining and carpet—all the inhabitants dangerously unaware that a single pinch of a lighter would be enough to fry the entire area into a chalk of salty ruins.

The grinding of tyres on the beaten track began and echoed, groaning across the barren field. Their heads turned. Out of a beaten car the ginger face emerged, smiling and at once ridiculously happy—the two qualities that Vince had managed to possess in his seventeen years of incumbent mediocrity.

Brett moved straight for passenger seat. Dana slipped into the back, noticing the suspension was uncomfortably low to the ground, and peered out the rotten windshield.

'Drinking, at 9am?' said Vince, taking the bottle. 'As your attorney—I approve of this decision.'

He was an infiltrator, Dana thought. A lecherous hawk, whose valued possessions amounted to a crate of beer and a packet of Dunny blues in the glovebox. He'd bought them fresh from the corner store, kicking his sneakers against the kerb. 'Can you believe the price of fags today? It's heinous. Absolutely fucking heinous, I say. It's the government that's done it—bloody National, the scum.'

They drove past Albany and Silverdale until they met Birkenhead. Down a long coiled road, in an apple-red Corolla, they drove. The high mesh fences obscured much of the pink factory, which was shining and ugly in the wainscoted sun. A few silver trucks peeled out of the drive, carrying the logo on the sides. Chelsea Sugar Factory. Since 1864.

It was warm for September. Baby swans were snuffling at the lapping water's edge, craning their beaks for their mothers and chirruping when they got the chance for bread. An Asian family were feeding the birds, the toddler dressed in plaid pull-ups and a hat and double-lace Crocs.

Vince pulled into the vacant lot, parking by a view of the harbour. It was crystalline and metal out there—the squats of Auckland glinting like metallic skyscrapers.

Dana opened the door and hoisted herself out of the no-lock.

'This your idea of a date, Brett?' she said.

He blushed. 'Of course not. This was Vince's idea. To have a look around.' He nodded in the direction of the Chelsea factory.

She glared at Vince. 'This your idea of a joke, Vince?'

'Just come on, will you?' he said. Vince never snapped. 'Just let me show you what's inside. Just give me a chance.'

Dana smirked. 'All right, but it better bloody be good.'

Vince led them to an opening in the fence, supporting himself up on a stumped kauri tree. He rolled over and landed in a rough patch.

'Fuck!' he hissed. 'Watch your step!'

They peeked inside the factory through the grimy windows. Puffs of steam pealed up to the roof-spike. Giant metal craters full of simmering sugar cane lined the room, boiling and bubbling.

Brett walked up to an iron mezzanine. Vince joined him, but Dana was still looking around.

'There's a story about this place,' said Vince, unamused. 'They say a sugar worker fell into one of those pots and boiled himself to death.'

Brett scowled. 'Not of his own choice, I take it?'

'It wasn't a suicide, no,' said Vince. 'But he died. And his ghost still haunts this place.'

'Explains the creepy vibes,' said Dana, joining them on the mezzanine.

She shook her legs out and sank into a cross-legged position, pressing her back against the cold framing.

'Hey!' Vince looked up as, out of the blue, a dark figure wearing aviators and a velvet top hat appeared and pushed him, suddenly and very hard, toppling him down the stairs and landing him in a bunched heap at the bottom.

'What the fuck, Vince?' said Dana, and she raced down to him.

A bone was jutting out of a strange place at the ankle, bulged up like a bloated mandrake and turning purpled-blue.

'Fuck's sake,' she said, examining the damage. 'He's broken it. He needs a hospital.'

'What happened?' asked Brett. 'What happened? Did you just slip or—'

'I—I was pushed!' glared Vince. 'I was *pushed* down the stairwell by that bastard in a top hat!'

'What?'

'That man,' he said, his eyes roving about wildly. 'Didn't you see him? He shoved me down the fucking stairs!'

But neither Brett nor Dana knew what he was talking about. They exchanged a glance, nervously, and Dana muttered, 'Let's get out of here.'

At the Auckland emergency department, Vince was pushed back in a nursing bed, enjoying the slow sedate of the morphine drip. They had brought him takeaways from the tuck downstairs. He bunched a salty fist around his next mouthful of chips and said, 'Well, that was exciting, wasn't it?'

'Terrifying,' Dana corrected. 'Terrifying is the adjective, Vince.'

'I still don't understand,' said Brett. 'What exactly happened to you out there? I looked around before we left but I didn't see anybody in a top hat. Nobody, Vince.'

Vince frowned. He licked his chops and took another fistful.

'Well that may be what you say, but I still say I saw him.'

Brett and Dana left Vince in the ED overnight. On their drive back, they stopped off at a servo outside Kaipara, outside the flats of Death Valley road.

Dana bought a blue Powerade and grumbled at the cashier. 'Why do all

Powerade ads revolve around sport? They need to show more baked geezers getting 2 for 1 after a big night out.'

The cashier looked glum. In the forecourt, a man in a cowboy hat was sitting on the fender of a red ute, smoking. The smoke curled in effluvia and gusted out into the night. Dana glanced at him. He grinned a toothless grin.

'Brett,' she started.

'Yeah?' he said

'Let's get out of here, okay?'

They piled into the car and Dana locked the doors quickly. 'I don't know about you, blood diamond, but that guy out there—I didn't like the way he was looking at us.'

Brett frowned and turned his eyes back over his shoulder. 'What d'you mean?'

'Just the way he held his glance is all.' She fumbled with the ignition. 'It's nothing—I'm sure of it.'

Out on the road, whisking along the ever-darkening highway, Dana saw a flutter, and a glare appeared in the rear-view mirror. It was the cowboy in the red ute. He was speeding full behind them, his lights on high beam. He drove up alongside to overtake them, and suddenly they saw the aviator glasses. He pulled in front, causing Dana to slam on the brakes and fishtail. The Corolla hurtled side over into a ditch.

The wheels turned round and around again, and smoke poured up into the air.

'Robert Johnson met the devil on the crossroads,' Dana thought as she saw the X-curved junction through the shattered windscreen.

'Sugar Town' started blaring on the radio. The station must have come on by itself. Brett had a fuzzed gash—temple to nose—and was bleeding out torrents of blood.

Nobody's born evil though, she thought.

Nobody.

STEPHEN COATES

The Stone in My Shoe

I have only a vague idea what karma is, but apparently mine is bad. At least that's what Dee said as she squashed her hairdryer into her suitcase. She also made some disparaging remarks about my housekeeping, though I didn't understand what my furniture arrangements had to do with my less than illustrious life. I suspected it was all hippy bullshit. Still, something had to change, even I could see that.

I first learned about relaxation spaces in the supermarket. Two Merivale housewives talking in high-pitched voices in the delicatessen. The shorter one was explaining how fifteen minutes a day in her space helped her deal with the moods of someone called Malcolm. I didn't know any Malcolms but I did know quite a few Dicks so it seemed worth a try. I trailed after them down the frozen foods aisle, past the pasta sauce and breakfast cereal, just far enough away not to be accused of stalking.

My spare bedroom would be ideal. Small, quiet, with the only window looking out on the fence so there would be no distractions. The perfect place to regain my inner harmony. I think that's the phrase she used. Unfortunately a toddler chose that moment to throw a tantrum by the chocolate biscuits and I couldn't hear all that clearly.

I'd forgotten how untidy it was. Getting rid of clutter, that's crucial. The blonde woman in Big Fresh was very firm on that point. Jan, her name was, or Jean. I thought of her as my peace-of-mind guru. I put away my winter clothes, dusted, vacuumed, stacked the cardboard boxes in the top of the cupboard. I was impressed with myself. Dee would have been too, though she wouldn't have admitted it. I was ready. Satori, here we come. I sat cross-legged in the gap between the bed and the desk, placed my hands lightly on my knees, palms up, thumb and forefinger forming a circle of life. Just like they do in the kung fu movies.

What a waste of time that was. The instant I closed my eyes I heard the ticking of the clock. I tried to ignore it but the damn thing drove me crazy. I opened one eye and glared at it. I swear it started ticking louder just to spite me. I took the battery out and stuffed it in my back pocket. That was no good either, because as soon as I sat down again it jabbed into my buttock like the princess and her bloody pea. I tossed it in the oddments drawer in the kitchen. Resumed the lotus position, smirking at the silent clock. It could never defeat me because I was smarter. I exhaled and waited for serenity. But the clock's malevolent mechanical brain was still thinking about making a noise. Ticking silently, as it were. I took it out back and smashed it with a hammer.

It was time for some serious tidying. I emptied the wardrobe, filling a council rubbish bag with old calendars, heavy metal posters, tacky ornaments and toys of unknown origin. My ghetto blaster, Playstation 2 and as-seen-on-TV exercise machine went at the back of the carport. Maybe someone would do me a favour and pinch them.

The desk was slightly off centre so I pulled it a few inches to the right. Then I fretted about symmetry. My uncle, a keen photographer, once told me the focal point should never be in the middle of the picture. I pushed it a foot the other way. That was better, I thought, though I didn't have much confidence in my judgement. Dee would have known. She was good at stuff like that. Then I noticed the indentations left by the legs, four square blemishes in the carpet. I pulled the desk back where it started.

The painting was wrong too. I took it down but all I got was a bunch of unsightly holes in the wall. Then I realised it wasn't mine and I didn't like it—and did I really need a cheap reproduction of some dead bloke I'd never heard of to remind me how uncultured I was? I had a girlfriend for that. Or I used to. In the end I broke it up with an axe, burned it in the fireplace.

The bed—that had to go. Unless I was planning to use it, which would be dumb. My goal was meditation, not a nap. I dragged the mattress onto the lawn where I could worry about it later. Then I hunted out an adjustable wrench and undid the bolts. That was fun. I like undoing things. I dismantled the desk as well.

There was no question it was an improvement, with no furniture or decoration to get in the way of fulfilment of my true self. I took several deep breaths, blowing out in approved yoga fashion. Then I sat on the floor and tried to relax. After thirty seconds I turned ninety degrees, away from the window. A minute later I moved again. Soon I had done a complete circle, a failure in every direction.

The crack in the windowpane, courtesy of my former flatmate Barry and eight bottles of India pale ale, had never bothered me before, but now it was a small triangle of imperfection in my flawless room. Then I began to see all the other ugly marks—worn patches in the carpet, stains from old cellotape and Blu-Tack, the dent where the door handle hit. A tiny cartoon dinosaur in purple felt. (It wasn't me, I promise.)

I got a man in to fix the glass. He couldn't fit me in until a week on Thursday. In the meantime I ripped up the carpet, breaking my fingernails in the process, and took it to the dump. Bought a Black and Decker and a pair of goggles and sanded back the floorboards. Even wearing a mask, by the end of the day my nostrils were thick with dust. Then, after vacuuming, wiping and washing, I painted the whole floor with three coats of polyurethane. I figured the headache was a small price to pay.

It took me four days to paint the walls. Salmon pink was not conducive to relaxation. I picked the blandest white I could find in the hardware store. After filling in the holes in the plaster with Polyfilla I gave it one layer of undercoat and two top coats. Even the act of using the roller was satisfying. Enlightenment and satisfaction probably aren't the same but I enjoyed it anyway. Once I'd finished I spent the afternoon lying in a beanbag watching the paint dry.

Third time's a charm. I shaved, showered, brushed my teeth. Put on clean clothes—running shorts and a cotton t-shirt. Then I lowered myself onto a thin cushion angled towards the plainest corner. Wriggled around a bit to get comfortable and closed my eyes.

Something was off. I held the position long after it became clear it wasn't going to work. I didn't whimper. I definitely didn't whimper, though I may have let out a faint moan. I rocked back and forth on the mat, covering my face. Then I tipped forwards and banged my head against the woodwork. What had gone wrong?

It didn't come to me in a blinding flash. I'm not a blinding flash sort of guy. Instead it crept up on me gradually, worming into my conscious mind. There was one way to find out. My knees creaked as I stood. In the kitchen I weighed my keys in my hand. Wrinkled my nose while I thought, then dropped them back in the basket. The front door clicked when I pulled it shut behind me. Down the steps, across the grass, along the narrow path at the side of the house. Stopped with my feet in the bark chips and rested my chin on the windowsill as I peered inside. There was no doubt about it. It was perfect.

HELEN VIVIENNE FLETCHER

Mondegreen

Jenny,
I love you. I'm sorry.
Marco

Marco's CDs sat in three boxes on the floor of Jenny's bedroom. The first box was all mainstream bands. Mostly rock and pop.

The Goo Goo Dolls.
Matchbox Twenty.
Daniel Cage.
Owl City.
Silverchair.

Marco was the one who told Jenny that if you listened to Black Sabbath backwards, you didn't get satanic messages—you got a recipe for cake in French. She spent three hours typing different versions of what she could hear into Google Translate before she realised he'd made it up.

Marco had felt pretty bad about that, especially as Jenny had ruined her dad's record player by running it backwards over and over.

A couple of days after that, Marco had turned up at her house with a new needle for it. She found out later he'd stolen it from his brother's shop. Marco never told his brother about it and neither did Jenny. She was pretty sure he knew, though. Every time she went over there he'd give her dirty looks, right up until the day of the funeral. He didn't look at her at all that day.

Peter kissed Jenny for the first time the day after Marco's funeral. Partly because they were both grieving, but partly because it was inevitable. They had been circling each other like hunting dogs for weeks now.

Jenny kissed him back, only because she knew that had been what she wanted before Marco died. She felt Peter's hand against the back of her neck, his palm warm and rough. She remembered the time she had got drunk at a friend's party and Marco had held her hair back for her as she threw up.

'People in drunk houses shouldn't throw beers,' he'd said. She'd laughed, even though it didn't make sense. His hands had been soft against her skin.

Jenny wasn't sure what she wanted now. She just kept shaking her head, as if that would somehow change things.

The second box was the indie bands. The alternative ones. And the bands whose genre varied, depending on where the store manager chose to place them, or on the mood of iTunes on any given day.

Filter.

Dashboard Confessional.

Death Cab for Cutie.

Bush.

Our Lady Peace.

Marco and Jenny used to listen to CDs together. He'd text her, or she'd text him, and they'd both press play at the same time.

Jenny liked that they'd fall asleep listening to the same songs.

After he died, Jenny would still send the texts. Opshop, she'd say and then she'd press play. Sometimes she'd wait for him to text back. The CD would whirr into silence, but still her phone wouldn't beep.

Jenny played his favourite albums. The ones she didn't really like but had listened to just for him. He knew, and had hardly ever suggested those ones, even though Jenny knew sometimes that was what he wanted to hear. Just like Jenny had never suggested Florence and the Machine, even though she loved them. She hadn't listened to their album in months now.

Marco's mum gave Jenny all of his CDs. She said Jenny would appreciate them the most. Marco's mum didn't know that neither Jenny nor Marco ever bought an album without making sure the other got a copy too.

'I bought you a present,' Peter said, the first day Jenny came back to school after Marco died. He handed her an MP3 player. 'I thought it would be easier.'

Jenny turned the bright-pink, glorified flash drive over in her hand. She thought of trying to explain how she and Marco had grown up running in and out of Marco's brother's shop. That they had spent every moment they could playing the cassette tapes, and records and CDs until his brother would drive them out. That the CDs had been a choice, not an inconvenience.

'Pink's my favourite colour,' she said instead, and thanked Peter politely for the gift. Then she put the MP3 player in the back of her locker and closed the door on it.

Marco had left Jenny a letter. That was why he was out that night, in the dark, in the rain. He was riding home from her house, where he had left the letter in the mailbox.

For a while, Jenny thought maybe it was a suicide note—that he had ridden his bike into the path of the truck on purpose. She didn't tell anyone about this idea. She pushed it to the back of her mind and let it fester there.

The third box contained mix CDs, ones Marco had made himself. Some were marked with Jenny's name, some with Marco's own.

None of them were marked with playlists.

Jenny opened the box once. She looked at the disks with her name on and wondered why he had never given them to her.

Then she shut the box and never opened it again.

Jenny,

I want you to know I'm sorry. I want you to know this isn't your fault. I want you to know ...

Jenny,

I don't know what I can say. You're my best friend. I've loved you since the moment I met you. That day at school when you sat down and tipped my crayons out across the desk? I wish I could go back to that moment. I wish I'd picked them up for you. Instead I think you cried when they all rolled off the table, and ... none of this is what I'm really trying to say.

I'm sorry, Jenny, I'm so ...

Jenny,

I've tried so many times to write this, and each time I screw the paper up before I finish. What is there I can say?

I sent you a text tonight and you didn't reply. You're probably just asleep. You probably didn't hear your phone, but I can't help thinking you don't want to talk to me.

About today—if you want to go out with Peter then that's fine. I want you to be happy. You need to know, though, that I love you. I've always loved you.

I wish I could say that face to face.

I guess it doesn't matter now, anyway. I guess none of this matters.

I'm sorry, Jenny, I'm so sorry. I wish ...

Jenny smoothed the letters out over her knees. They were on blue notebook paper, like the letter he had left in her mailbox. On the bottoms of the pages there was an imprint from something else written on the same pad. It looked like lyrics, probably from a song they had both loved. She could only make out one fragment of a line though: *let you go.*

Marco's brother sat next to Jenny, watching her read the letters. She had wanted to take them home and read them alone, sucking each of the words from the page until they became a part of her soul. Instead she read them there and then, sitting in silence with Marco's brother as they tried to pretend the only thing joining them wasn't gone.

'I found them in his rubbish bin,' he said.

Jenny nodded. The pages were creased from having been balled up.

'I guess he never—'

'No,' Jenny said. 'He never told me.'

'Well …' Marco's brother's voice trailed off into a sigh. His name was Steven. Steve. Jenny would never think of him as that, though. He would always be 'Marco's brother'.

There were many things she could have said to him. She could have apologised for the stolen record player needle. She could have thanked him for giving her the letters. She could have asked him if he had been the one to pack up Marco's CDs—the one to meticulously arrange them by genre, and whether he knew what was on the mix CDs.

Or she could have asked him whether he had the same idea festering in the back of his mind as she did in hers.

Instead they sat in silence.

Both of them thinking about Marco.

Marco's favourite song was 'Everything You Want' by Vertical Horizon.

Jenny didn't remember when he told her that. She hoped she didn't laugh at him, or scoff or anything like that. She couldn't imagine that she would have, but the fact that she couldn't remember made it feel like she must have blocked it out.

She must have listened to that song so many times without really hearing the lyrics. It was a song about a boy who loved a girl. A song about a girl who didn't love him back. Now when Jenny listens to it, she gets it.

She wished she could remember the moment he told her about that song.

She wished she could remember the moment he had tried to tell her, and she hadn't heard him. Did he stare at her, waiting for her to understand? Did he press play and walk away, and just hope that she'd make sense of the lyrics herself?

Or maybe he just texted it to her.

Maybe he just texted her the same song so many times she figured out it was his favourite without him having to say so.

Jenny taped Marco's letters to the underside of her bed. She laid them one on top of the other, in the order she thought he had written them. The letter he had left in her mailbox was on top.

Jenny,

I love you. I'm sorry.

Marco

Then she penned her own letter—what she would have said to him if he had told her. She taped her letter facing his, so the lines could read each other.

The day Marco died, he had yelled at Jenny. She'd been late to meet him because she had wanted to walk home with Peter. Jenny had meant to text him to say she was going to be late, but she'd forgotten. Instead she sat outside the classroom, where Peter was stuck in detention, while Marco sat at her place waiting for her to come home.

She and Peter walked together and, by the time they got to her place, she had forgotten she'd been supposed to meet Marco.

'Do you want to come in?' Jenny had smiled at Peter and fluttered her eyelashes in a way she was ashamed of now.

Peter had grinned and followed her inside.

Marco was sitting at the kitchen counter. He smiled when Jenny opened the door, but then his face crumpled as he saw Peter.

'Marco, I meant to—'

He shook his head and grabbed his jacket.

'I'm sorry, I—'

'Forget it. Just forget it.'

'Marco!' She could see he was crying. She reached out but he pushed her away.

'Are you blind or are you just stupid?' He brushed his tears away, as if he was angry with himself for crying.

Jenny shook her head. 'I don't—'

'You're not stupid. You're just selfish, aren't you, Jenny?' Marco nodded to Peter. 'Go on. Why don't you go off and sleep with him? Act like a slut like the rest of the girls at school.'

Peter pushed Marco then. Jenny's face burned and she couldn't look at either them. Instead she locked herself in the bathroom and cried. When she came out, both Marco and Peter were gone.

That night Jenny heard her phone beep. She knew it would be Marco.

She didn't answer.

She texted Marco Vertical Horizon, and then pressed play. From her drawer, she heard his cellphone beep, but she covered her ears against the sound.

She tried to pretend Marco was at his house, pressing play, falling asleep listening to the same song as her.

MARTHA MORSETH

A Modern Look at the Seven Deadly Sins

i. Constant companions
After a lunch of pasta and iced coffee
a slice of ginger crunch to finish off
she meets her friend in a café
noted for double chocolate muffins.
This afternoon is special; the friend
is in town only for today and the food so enticing
chocolate éclairs, black forest slices
how can she refuse?
After an affogato it's back to work and late home
to left-over cream pie waiting.
One piece she promises herself
before the pizza
and another night of TV.

ii. Keeping up
Over a hundred thousand dollars he paid
a good down payment for a house at the beach.
He has that, too, and him making no more than me
probably family money, a bundle I reckon
with expensive vacations each year and skiing
an airplane in his back garden next
maybe his wife has a packet stashed overseas.
Even with my missus working it's hard to keep up.
'As long as we have each other,' she says.
Well, we've got each other and three hungry mouths.
I look at his driveway, can picture me at the wheel
there'd be a low growl, a quick getaway, a rush of wind
on the open road.

iii. Solipsism

A woman I barely know smiles, nods in greeting
while I drink my coffee, goo-goos at the baby
strapped to her belly.
The infant thrashes its hands at the sugar bowl,
cups, the milk jug which it grabs to its face
along with a paper serviette.
  'So sensitive,' the woman says when the child bites
the paper into ragged pieces with its gummy mouth.
'He likes to touch, to feel the nature of things with his lips.
The doctor says he's very advanced for his age.'
  The neonate delinquent grabs a spoon,
bangs it on the table. I offer my hand to distract. It cries,
looks at Mum.
  The woman lifts the whiny bundle from her lap,
says, 'Did that strange lady scare you? Doesn't she know
you're the most beautiful baby in the whole, wide world?'
  I push back my chair, mumble goodbye. On the street
I glance back. Through the thick window of distorted glass
I see the child's mouth screaming.

iv. Watching

Men's legs
the strong, muscled ones
lightly covered with fine blond hairs
catching the sun.
She sees them on the beach
on the street in shorts
their tendons taut to leap in sport or rush her away
for an afternoon of playful love
on the white sheets of her narrow bed
overlooking a garden of flowering kowhai
his legs dissolving in golden clouds.

v. Possibilities

The young female
wears black stilettos
a gossamer top that catches the breeze
thigh-hugging skirt
smoke-lens glasses
Blonde hair piled into a dishevelled knot—
from an afternoon tryst?
    The woman on her lunch break
sitting near the café's large window
sips her coffee. Watches.
Decides to pick up hair dye after work
try on shoes from a nearby mall
do the op shops tomorrow for chiffon and crêpe
won't have the caramel slice after all.

vi. Meltdown

Godawful day. Hot as hell. Perspiration under my arms, down my back. Traffic crawls through the supermarket carpark, coagulates into lines of shiny metal under the yellow sodium lights.

    Maybe I'll get lucky, catch a car leaving, glide right in. An empty place ahead—taken by a dirty grey Subaru; the next space—a black Toyota full of kids. Another lane, nearly scrape a dented Ford.

    God, it's hot with the air conditioner out. A gap ahead but a Porsche takes it. Rich bastard. Go around again. More bloody cars push in. I clench the steering wheel, grind my teeth, rev the motor at a green Holden outmanoeuvring me. The woman driver smiles, mouths 'Sorry'. I could punch her.

    The next park's got to be mine. I turn the corner. A dark van backs out. I swing in first and as I do, I feel a jolt. A monster SUV behind me, bull bars touching my boot, headlights glaring.

    The heavy-set man behind the wheel roars, 'You took my slot, Dipshit!' I get out, look at my car, a dent as big as the guy's bald head. He pulls away. I race after, beat on his window, scream, 'If I see you here again, Arsehole, you're dead. You hear me? DEAD!'

vii. Dissipating the day
is one sin I do well, beginning with newspaper
toast and tea in bed hours after sun-up. More
reading or sleep until I shower, not often.

    I wear clothes from the day before; it's easier
than making decisions. I might play a video game
or meet a friend if the car has enough gas.

    I order books online or wait for the book bus
drink a lot of coffee, shuffle through bills, comb
my hair if I can be bothered to find a comb.

    After tea I watch TV or play more games
ignore phone messages, don't invite friends over
as I'd have to tidy the house.

    I could hire a someone to wash the
cobwebbed windows but I can live with dirty views.

Key to the Sins: i. gluttony, ii. greed, iii. pride, iv. lust, v. envy, vi. wrath, vii. sloth.

JOANNA PRESTON

Anxiety

It's assembled of all the leavings,
shredded and ground down and layered
—this hang-up phone call, that
strange lump—the dark sweepings
from corners you'd rather not see
(the hint of a whiff from the basement
at breakfast, that flash of a face
in the crowd). It needs
turning over, now and again,

and again now it needs to be stirred,
to be aired, to be stoked so the stench
will dissipate, the alchemical heat
of decomposition seep in
to the night air—some sort
of contagion.

This you know, deep in the bone:
the compost beneath every throne.

OWEN MARSHALL

A Night with Strangers

Serious illness made the future less secure, and Robert tended to retreat into the past, which in general had been kind to him. He spent a lot of time sorting the family photographs, the earlier ones already in albums, but most loose, or still stored just on the computer.

He wanted to annotate them—names, dates and places—so they would remain meaningful years later. Already some were a puzzle even to him, and could have been palmed into the files by a complete stranger.

Especially this was true of the images taken on their overseas trips: vistas, classical ruins and quaint cobbled streets that evoked no more personal feelings than postcards, or the illustrations in a travel magazine. Those he did recognise conveyed a sense of transience, almost of loss, as he saw their earlier, more robust selves smiling at him from the past.

Some of the people had since died, some captured in the background of the photographs were utter strangers, as in a shot taken at Delphi that had in the left corner by a colonnade a fat man with walk socks, glancing their way with a self-deprecating smile. Just for that moment he was on the periphery of their lives, but transfixed there by the camera as a sign that he too had existed. His physical appearance was detailed, even to the sweat patches on his shirt, but his life a mystery.

Some of the most familiar pictures, however, acted like swipe cards and opened up whole rooms of memory. Robert found one of long-time friends Phil and Harriet standing together outside their house in Dunedin, and it brought back to him an oddity of experience that kept him silent at the table while a sun-shower drifted across the city, and Susan tried to convince herself that things were okay by the repetition of trivial and customary domestic tasks.

Phil and Harriet had just moved to Invercargill and their Dunedin house was empty. Robert was to attend a conference at the dental school, and his friend invited him to stay at their former place. He could have gone to a motel. It wasn't the money, though in those days that was a consideration; Phil seemed keen to help, and sometimes it's a strengthening thing in a friendship to accept a kindness.

'The new people aren't moving in until the weekend,' Phil had said. 'The power's still connected although the phone's off.'

'Thanks, but I'll get a motel. It's only for the night,' Robert had said.

'Just take a sleeping bag and turn the water on. We did a deal and some of the furniture's still there. The key's on the nail under the garage window.'

So after the meeting in the afternoon Robert drove to St Kilda, let himself in and turned on the water heating. The house was rather forlorn, as if it realised that the family it had protected for many years had callously abandoned it. Robert and Susan had visited often, and its hollow silence seemed strange to him. The house seemed vulnerable, like a woman caught still in her dressing gown and with hair undone. Most of the lounge furniture was gone, leaving small indentations in the carpet and a red wine stain that had been hidden by the sofa. Harriet had cleaned the kitchen drawers and left them to dry, stacked on the bench. On the sills of the sunniest windows were a few dead flies, like currants against the white surface.

He could have spread his sleeping bag on what he knew had been the marriage bed, but instead chose one of the other rooms. He walked to the Thai restaurant and brought back a takeaway that he ate in the kitchen where there were still the table and six chairs.

Normally he took milk, but he just used one of the tea bags from his case and sat with the mug at the table, looked over the agenda points for the next morning, and then rang Susan on his cellphone, aware of the unusual taste of the tea as they talked.

'So how's the place looking?' she asked.

'A bit sad and empty, though the kitchen's still got table and chairs, and they must have sold the beds and mattresses to the people as well.'

'They came to an arrangement about the curtains and blinds, Harriet told me. Good on her. None of the old stuff would really fit a new place, would it?' Robert hadn't noticed the curtains. 'When you're back make sure you ring and thank them. It would be great if they could come up some time. Invercargill's such a long way away.'

'How's Donna?'

'She misses you. Sharon came over after school and they vanished into her room as usual, just coming out to ask for something to eat.' An easy pause. 'I miss you too,' Susan said.

In the southern summer the twilight is long, and after the call he'd sat and watched the shadows gather in the garden. There is a special and passing moment at dusk when, although the external light is fading, the colours of the flowers seem softly illuminated from within to form an aura. Sometimes the two families had come together for a barbecue in the garden, and although Robert tired of Harriet going on about her kids, they were good times and good friends. Susan was right. It would be great to see them again.

He'd decided to have a shower, but the water had barely warmed and he ducked in and out, not shampooing his hair. Even before he'd dried himself there was a hammering at the front door. Robert tied the towel around his waist and went down the hall towards the uncouth and moving shapes he could see behind the stippled glass. He didn't open the door fully, and kept his body hidden. Four people crowded towards him: a middle-aged couple in front and a younger pair behind.

'May I bloody well ask who you are?' It was the older man who spoke: short, thin and with a ploughshare of a nose. The woman beside him was taller, fuller, and her neck trembled with the tension of the moment. Robert explained as best he could, and as he talked the edging pressure of the foursome forced him back until the door was open and all of them in the hall.

'I come to our new home,' said the man in a theatrical astonishment despite Robert's story. 'I come to our new home to find the key gone and a naked guy inside. Jesus.'

'The Snowdens said you were taking possession at the weekend. It was all okay by them for me to stay one night.'

'The house is ours, signed and sealed. We come to it and find a naked guy living here.'

'Well, I'm not actually naked, am I? Just coming from a quick shower so I grabbed a towel. I can get dressed and buzz off in no time if that's what you want.'

But having taken possession of the moral high ground and established that Robert had a connection to the previous owner, the small man was no longer confrontational.

'Now you're here you might as well stay on,' he said with conscious largesse. 'Too late to go off finding somewhere now.' He introduced himself: Terence, his wife Mary, his son (something that sounded like Binge), and Binge's girlfriend, Amber. Binge was as short and spare as his father, but his nose was still growing so his features were in pleasant enough transitional balance. Amber was a head taller and a full cheek wider at the arse of her jeans. She would end a fat woman, but in the present could pass as voluptuous in a slightly ungainly way. Amber had a shy, low voice and a lovely smile, as women with full faces often do.

Robert had never met a Terence; surely no people alive had the name. While Robert put his clothes on, the others carried in blankets, a couple of suitcases and a chilly bin. They took the six kitchen chairs into the empty lounge. When he came back in, Robert wondered if there was to be a further member of the family. Terence and Mary put their blankets in the main bedroom and Binge his and Amber's in the room next to Robert's. They were going to spend a couple of days, Terence explained. A sort of tester of the new place, he said.

It was awkward at first: the five of them sitting on kitchen chairs and with nowhere to rest their arms, not even a table. Robert was the odd man out, but in the circumstances he couldn't go to bed without a minimum of social interaction. He enquired as to Terence's job, was introduced to the workings of the drainage board, and he asked a question that included the word reticulation. Good man, he congratulated himself. He didn't forget Binge.

'And what about you? What's your line, Binge?' He fudged the name because he wasn't sure if he had it right, but Binge made no correction. Turned out he was a helicopter pilot, and had been all over the place, even Colombia. Turned out he'd met Amber only three weeks before when she'd taken a scenic flight from Queenstown. Amber was from Adelaide and taking a break from her media studies at a polytech there.

She and Binge were more interesting than Terence and Mary. Mary didn't do anything at all as far as Robert could make out, though she did have a rare condition that meant her toenails had fallen out, and more than once.

Binge said he was tired, and he and Amber went off before ten o'clock. Robert thought that was his opportunity, but Terence made it clear that he had something of import to say.

'You'll want to hear this,' said Mary, and even straightened somewhat in the kitchen chair.

'Terence Berne, Terence Berne,' he said slowly and with an intent look at Robert. 'It doesn't ring any bells?' He leant towards Robert as if proximity would encourage recall, as if his face should strike recognition.

'I don't think so, no.' Terence's nose was more like a muzzle, really, but his teeth were sound for a man of his age, and he had a good head of hair.

'The child in the stormwater drain at Tainui?' said Terence significantly.

'No, sorry.'

'It was news all over the country,' Terence insisted. 'On TV and everything.'

'He was interviewed,' said Mary. 'He would've got a bravery medal except several had already been nominated that year. Any other year he would've got an award, the superintendent said.'

'It burns into your soul it does, something like that. You never forget it,' said Terence.

'Being a child makes it that much worse, doesn't it?' added Mary.

'You can't forget such a thing,' repeated Terence.

'Being a child and all, too,' said his wife.

'Seven years old,' said Terence, and he was off on the story that was the defining moment of his life. All about the call-out, and the manhole cover off, and the girl's body face down with the parting in her hair between the braids bone-white in the dimness. As he listened, Robert thought he remembered the tragedy, although it was years ago. An instance of the bestiality that is revealed in society from time to time.

'He had two weeks' special leave because of it,' said Mary. 'We went up to my sister in Nelson who's passed on now. She was always closest to me in the family, although not nearest in age.'

'You carry it always,' said Terence with a tinge of heroic dignity. He was disappointed that Robert didn't recognise him, and consequently thought less of him as a companion for conversation. Robert was able to say goodnight.

'I'll be out of your hair early tomorrow,' he said.

He didn't sleep well, being awoken at two and again at five by tempestuous lovemaking in the next room. It's never comforting to lie alone at night and hear the physical pleasures of others. Amber worked up to a sort of pulsating moan that was synchronised with the loud workings of the bed. Her noise was almost unbearably sexual and quite involuntary, brimming with ecstasy and submission at the same time. Robert couldn't get to sleep again after the second bout, even when the house was quiet. Binge might have been a helicopter pilot, but he was surely never closer to heaven than when clasped to Amber.

By seven, Robert was dressed and packed, hoping to slip away without disturbing the family, but although Amber and Binge were no doubt in deep, sated slumber, Terence and Mary were in the lounge eating marmalade toast, and in muted dispute over a colour scheme for the kitchen. Their single point of agreement was that the existing yellow walls were intolerable.

'You just got to be practical in a kitchen, don't you?' said Terence. His nose seemed slightly enlarged, though he may well have been telling the truth.

'The kitchen's not the place to get all house and garden,' said Mary. 'Yellow's for a sunroom or conservatory.'

'Practicality, see?' emphasised Terence, 'cause there's all that plumbing, and work stations and storage. Yellow's not a colour for any of those, you'd have to say, wouldn't you?'

'I have to be on my way,' said Robert. 'Thanks again for putting up with me. Much appreciated. I'm sorry Phil got muddled about when you were going to take possession.'

'No harm done,' said Terence. 'These mix-ups happen.'

Terence and Mary even came to the door to watch him walk to his rental car. The same door that showed clearly behind Phil and Harriet in the photograph Robert now held. He had to make a mental effort to break from memory and return to the present.

'We never see Phil and Harriet now,' he said to Susan.

'What made you think of them?' She was testing the seal on the home-made chutney that was the gift from the previous day's visitors.

'This photograph,' he said, holding it up. Susan came to his shoulder, put on her glasses and took the photograph. Robert was about to start talking about Terence and family, but his wife had no connection with them and he couldn't be bothered establishing their invisible presence in the picture.

'I stayed a night there once after they'd moved out,' was all he said, referring to their friends.

'When you're feeling better,' she said, 'we'll take a trip and catch up with them and others as well. They still send cards, you know.' She gave the snap back.

Robert looked again at the house with its glass-panelled front door and the Snowdens smiling as they stood before it. He half expected Terence to appear behind them, nosing forward, eager to recount again his experience of tragedy.

CHRISTINA STACHURSKI

From *The Stone Women*

I

A driveway swept up along a clipped hedge and sheared to the right through shadowed trees. Izzy changed down further on the gravel, drove around into an opening full of sun and the house, double-storeyed and huge. She parked the Holden next to the portico and ran up the steps to push open the heavy front door. It was dim in the wood-panelled hall. Yellow light, thick with dust, filtered through faraway windows above the landing. There was a faint smell of old rubbish. Footsteps rushed over the ceiling and Connor appeared, coming down the stairs two at a time.

'Saw the car out the window—nice. Hey.' He hugged her. 'You finally made it.' Izzy hugged back hard. They were pushed apart by a surfboard nosing through an opening door.

'Sorry,' mumbled someone through toast, who looked up briefly. 'Out to Taylors, man?'

Connor shook his head, inclined it towards Izzy. Sinbad focused and his eyes widened. 'Geez, look at the hair—has to be the sister,' he said, wiping butter and crumbs on his shirt and sticking his hand out. 'Much better looking.'

'Izzy—Sinbad,' said Connor. 'See you tonight, Sin. My shout.'

'Right. Slater mate.'

'Come on up,' said Connor. At the top of the stairs there was another wood-panelled hall filled with doors. 'This is us,' he said, steering her through the second doorway on their left into an enormous room. Just inside, a carved wooden fireplace reached from floor to ceiling, its inset mirror reflecting a wide bay window and treetops outside.

'Like it,' said Izzy.

'And that's not all,' said Connor, crossing to open a pair of leadlight bevelled-glass doors. 'Here we have the bedroom with en suite and balcony.'

The bed squashed against three walls, tucked under a stained-glass window. An oak wardrobe and dresser crowded the rest of the room. Izzy caught sight of a framed black and white photograph. Gesturing towards it, she said, 'They'd be really proud of you.'

'Hope so,' said Connor. Izzy patted her brother's back. 'You can sit out here,' he said, and climbed through the bedroom's open sash window, held washing back so Izzy could see where she was going. They sat on deeply warm roof tiles, resting their feet on an arch over the window below. Izzy flicked Connor's red-gold dreads over his shoulder and hugged him side on.

'You're looking good, bro,' she said.

'Fit, fast and dangerous.'

'Not much like a good-boy-star-student.' She pushed a finger through one of the holes in his Rip Curl shirt. Connor shrugged.

'They can't argue with my marks. The suits even had a special session to celebrate me getting the scholarship. Wore one I got from the op shop down on the corner, maroon with flares.'

Izzy laughed. 'So where's uni from here?'

'Down through the trees there's the river. Well, stream, but everyone calls it the river. Uni's on the other side.'

'Can we go over later, find the art school?'

'Sure, the full tiki tour—here, uni, into town. Oh, later on, I've invited some of the neighbours for dinner at the Chinese down the road so you can meet them.'

'And I'll have the egg foo yong, thanks,' said Evie, flicking back her blonde hair. The waitress added up the number of orders, counted people around the table. Five. Satisfied, she moved off.

'Where's Joe?' asked Stella.

'Couldn't find him,' Connor said. 'Sinbad'll be along when he gets in.'

'Bloody good food here, Izzy,' said Toby, patting his stomach. 'They do takeaways. Fish'n'chips next door and the dairy on the corner—no need to cook.'

'Don't forget Charcoal Chicken down on Riccy Road,' said Connor.

'Cholesterol poisoning coming up,' said Evie. 'Ever heard of vegetables?'

'Don't you worry about our green intake, Mam,' said Toby.

'Important advice, Izzy,' said Connor. 'Never trust Tobes's baking. Last house party, his chocolate cake had pretty much everyone vomiting.'

'Yeah, but they had a high old time after expurgation,' said Toby.

'How many people live in the house?' asked Izzy.

'Heaps,' said Toby. 'Had to make the cake in a roasting dish.'

'Seventeen flats in the house,' said Stella. 'One or two in each and same for all the cottages.'

'Was it a farm in the old days?' Izzy wanted to know. Everyone looked at each other and shrugged.

'S'pose. Riccarton House was,' said Toby. 'They look sort of the same.'

'Kirkwood Ave's way quirkier,' said Stella. 'Even without all the murdered animal heads in the hall.'

Toby banged the table.

'Got it,' he said. 'I can do my history research assignment on 14 Kirkwood as a serial site. Yeah, first the imperialist upper-crust whitey farmers and now the rich landlord—Johnson'll love it. And I'll scan in a photo of me writing on my laptop on the grand piano. He's always going on about pianos as symbols of colonising culture.'

'I could take the photo if you like,' said Izzy.

'Yeah right,' said Stella. 'If you can find the piano through the ceiling-high pile of crap on top of it.'

'Hey, anyone seen the new person above me?' Toby frowned and ground his teeth. 'Been pacing round half the night, squeaking the boards something wicked.'

'That's next door to me—you know,' Connor said. 'Some old chick—haven't talked to her.'

'Steak with satay sauce?' Toby put his hand up. The waitress had her arms full. 'Chicken chop suey with cashews?' A face squashed against the window, the bell on the door tinged and Sinbad slid into the seat next to Izzy, looked at her in mock wonder.

'A beautiful woman who drives a 186? It is yours, parked in Connor's space?' he asked.

'Yeah,' said Izzy, her eyes lighting up. '65. Only two owners. It'd been in a farm shed out at Albany for twenty years. Brilliant on the open road down from Auckland.'

'Should have been, time the repairs took,' said Connor. 'She was supposed to get here a week ago.'

'Parts were a bit hard to get,' said Izzy.

'Worth the wait. I'm in love,' Sinbad told the whole table as he made the shape of the car in the air with his hands, grinned at Izzy and smacked his lips in a big kiss.

'Ahem, that's my sister, mate,' said Connor.

'Here, have a drink.' Sinbad filled everyone's glasses to the brim and lifted his own. 'To Connor,' he said. 'Have a great time and don't take any stick from the ivy-league Yanks.'

'And welcome to Izzy,' said Evie.

'And a new year at uni,' added Stella. 'A good one.'

Can't be worse than my last one, thought Izzy.

'Skull,' said Toby.

Later, they made their way home along Kirkwood Ave in the green dark. As they rounded the bend, an older woman with a dog was coming the other way.

'Hello, boy,' said Izzy. 'Beautiful lab!' The woman looked straight ahead and kept walking.

'Never mind,' said Sinbad, dropping on to all fours. 'You can pat me instead.'

'Woof,' said Toby as he jumped on his back. 'Gee up, Neddy.' Sinbad threw him off and chased him down the street and into number 14's long driveway. As they got to the end of the concrete and the beginning of the trees, Toby stopped them. 'Ssshh,' he said. Hedgehogs snuffled in the darkness. 'Geez, you should have heard them going for it the other night.' Toby's impression of mating hedgehogs crescendoed as they walked up a gravel path next to the old cottages. A light came and went through the trees, beckoning from above the back door to the big house. Someone stepped out, carrying a crate full of washing.

'Mate,' said Sinbad.

'Hey Joe,' said Evie.

'This is Izzy,' said Connor. 'Izzy—Joe. He lives underneath our floor.' Joe's hand was warm and dirty. He smiled and little sparks of light shot out from his green eyes. Cute, thought Izzy, before she caught herself.

'Coffee?' offered Toby generally as they went in the back door and through the narrow passage into the big hall.

Connor looked at his watch and then at Izzy. 'We'd better head up,' he said. 'Got to hit the airport at four. I still have to pack.'

Evie and Stella hugged Connor. Toby got him in a headlock as Sinbad lifted him by the seat of his jeans and they ran him around the hall whooping before falling into a rolling wrestle on the carpet.

'See you in December, man,' said Joe as he gave Connor a hand up.

'There you go,' said Connor as he and Izzy climbed the stairs. 'Toby and Sinbad to keep you entertained, Joe for help with anything Fine Arts, and Stella and Evie for that weird girl stuff. But watch them, those two go a bit crazy sometimes.'

The next afternoon, around in Clyde Road, Charlotte dug steadily on, enjoying the sun's fierce heat on her back. Henry and Portia followed behind, flicking up little clods and pouncing. McDuff panted in the shade of one of the oaks. Winter vegetable bed turned over, Charlotte took off her gloves and gumboots and went inside. Waiting for the jug to boil, she cut two big slices of fruitcake, then, with the latest *Plays & Players* under her arm, carried the tray out to sit under the wisteria.

McDuff left off biting water streamers from the rotating sprinkler to claim his piece of cake. The cats sprawled beneath the seat, exposing as much fur as possible to its cooling shadow. Charlotte became engrossed in reviews of the Royal Shakespeare Company's production of *The Winter's Tale* and marked pages to copy for her honours class. Cafetière empty, she put the magazine down and got up. She felt dizzy.

Don't be silly, she said to herself, but the whirling in her head got worse. Must be the heat, she thought, sitting back down and fanning herself with the magazine. Shouldn't be digging in that full sun. Not as young as I used to be.

'Just a quick rest before we feed the roses,' Charlotte told the others. She leant her head back and her eyelids drooped into sleep. Minutes and then hours ticked by as the sun gradually lowered in the sky. Woken by the drop in temperature, Charlotte had just enough time to fry some salmon and leftover potatoes before *Midsomer Murders* started. She settled into the couch with dinner on her knee and a bottle of chardonnay at hand. But by the third ad break she was finding it hard to concentrate. Half an hour later she had a headache. I'm never sick, she thought. And certainly not at the beginning of term. Perhaps an early night.

On the other side of the city, Kirsten stopped at a turn in the steps to look at the sweep of estuary and sea. She wished she could stay enveloped in the blue calm. Grit stung the back of her eyes. The ache through her chest and gut was heavy. More steps climbed and she reached a plateau of manicured lawn where a herringbone brick path edged with box and lavender led to the front door. Kirsten had to catch her breath before tapping with the brass lion's head.

'Lovely to see you, darling,' said Cynthia Eton-Edwards.

Kirsten closed her eyes against perfume and air-kisses. 'Everyone's in the formal lounge.' Cynthia led off down the hall. 'We do hope you'll be happy with us this year. Always have a little gathering to introduce the Writer to the staff.' Kirsten braced herself as she followed. The doorbell sounded behind them.

'Please excuse me,' said Cynthia.

Just inside the door to the lounge, Kirsten pretended to study a painting of white roses. Someone tapped her on the back. It was a man with an excessive moustache.

'Hi there. Mike Bachelor, American Lit.' He shook her hand, held on to it longer than necessary. Kirsten's mouth made the shape of a smile. The rest of her face felt stuck. Another man elbowed Mike to the side.

'Dick Moody the Poet,' he said. 'Red or white?' He offered a glass of each.

'No thanks, I'm driving,' said Kirsten.

'You've read my stuff then?' said Dick.

'Mm,' said Kirsten, who hadn't.

'Eleventh collection coming up this year,' he said, grinning. 'Gotta keep the punters happy.' He drained the red and started on the white, elbow angled to keep the other man back. Kirsten knew she should say something.

'So you teach poetry?'

'Yep, how to read it and how to write it.' Dick talked on about himself. Mike pushed closer and did the same. They talked over each other at her. Kirsten only needed to nod every once in a while.

From across the room, a woman watched them. Black leather trousers strained around her legs beneath a layered chiffon top, low cut at the front and plunging at the back. She downed her glass of pinot gris, grabbed another and joined the group.

'Tara Jones,' she said. The men ignored her. Tara pulled Kirsten by the arm. 'I'm writing a novel,' she said. 'Just got the last chapter to do and then you can give it a once-over and send it to your agent.'

'Really?' said Kirsten, stepping back. Cynthia picked up a bell from the crush of silver objects on a mahogany side table. The tinkling halted conversations in stages until someone shushed Dick.

'Dinner's ready on the front patio,' said Cynthia. 'Please go out and help yourselves.' Kirsten hung back. It would be at least another hour before she could politely leave. She shut her eyes and tiredness dragged through her. Make an effort, she told herself. Can't fall over at the starting line. In fact the rest of the evening wasn't too difficult since everyone wanted to say hello and tell her who they were, so she could mostly smile and nod until the general move to leave.

Most of the English staff were well pleased with their new Writer in Residence.

'Charming young woman,' said Professor Roland Barker to his wife as he drove her home in the Rover.

'Great tits,' said Dick to Mike as they stopped for a few après-party brandies at the Ruptured Duck.

Fucking bitch, thought Tara Jones as she followed Kirsten's car across the causeway in her red MG. Who does she think she is?

When Kirsten got home, she poured half a glass of gin and turned the taps on for a bath. Even if the flat hadn't been cheap and close to the university, she would have taken it for the bathroom. Blue and white Victorian tiles ran across the floor and halfway up the walls. The bath rose on ornate eagle-claw feet and had a view of tree tops and sky. Very different from the Portobello bathroom's pine and stainless steel with doors opening out to the bay.

She put on Jennifer Warnes' *Famous Blue Raincoat* and slid into the warm water, hipbones jutting through her skin. One hand held the gin up on the edge of the bath. The other hit hard at her abdomen as she thought about the night her life had crashed. They'd been out for dinner at High Tide. She'd suggested it to cheer up her husband who was very stressed at work—she'd thought. Matthew hadn't slept for nights, hardly ate anything at dinner, kept clenching and unclenching his fists around the cutlery. She'd suggested again that he see a doctor.

'Wouldn't do any good,' he'd said.

'Why not?'

He'd started to say something, then filled his glass instead, looked at her quickly and slid his eyes away.

'Sorry Kirsty … this is very hard … The thing is … I want children.'

'But—'

'I know.' He told her that his fortieth birthday and father's death, coming so close together, had set him thinking. He couldn't help it: now he wanted children more than anything.

'We can adopt,' Kirsten had said.

'My own children. A proper blood family.'

She'd gone completely cold, walked out of the restaurant, along the beach and kept walking most of that night. She got a cab home from the city as dawn broke over the sea. Her imminent writing residency in Christchurch changed from a plan for them to enjoy living in two cities for a year, speeding up or down the island to be together at weekends, into a new life on her own.

And now here she was, two days into it.

Water drained out of the bath as she poured another drink. The straight gin tasted like medicine, a cool blurry strength spreading inside.

Toby arrived home in the flat beneath her, heard Jennifer Warnes and winced. Man, he thought, where is that chick's sense of authenticity? He put Cohen on the turntable and turned it up for her elucidation.

TOM WESTON

Gift

Ten years. Returned to
where she'd picked out the glass bowl,

so precisely annealed
it might be a substitute for light—

a luminescent topaz filling the curve
in which we travel.

*

She knew the fire, again, of its deliverance,
the intense blister from which the bulb,

leavened with chemicals, emerges,
carrying its yolk, the forecasting of knowledge

seeding the exact moment
of imminence, intent upon that entry.

*

With the tool of its making, old metal
is pressed to the nurturing trade, the sure and

respected art of creation:
her uncles had possessed this gift of industry,

the certainty that, from metal, a working life
would honour their possession of it.

*

The island stands proud of the sea.
Yet, in a careless glance, it might be thought

there is no land,
only buildings standing like reeds in

the lagoon, nature seeding sky, as metal oxides
borrow from the azure

*

and make their brief run for it,
persuaded this is not perfection,

or not only perfection, but some
simulacrum of an earlier anticipation,

certain that in this foundry
the bruised will bend its form to suit.

*

The glum and slightly dull glimmer of red
in its jellied helmet, the pelmet over

four tentacles, draped careless cords
swinging in the tide's ferment, undulation

through water is not random;
deception the preferred mode of address.

★

Medusa pumps through the
turquoise shallows, seeking to mark the skin

with its intense brand, to burn
a particular claim on what it knows.

Fire and poison, the whip-like
welt that blisters all it holds, singeing

★

its mark into the ready flesh, precursor or creator.
Fire attends thus to perfection,

bruise to healing; flesh
is scarred with yesterday's seed.

A gift of glass fit for the sea's memory.
The delivered fire obedient to her narration.

ELIZABETH SMITHER

Three 'Willow' Pattern Bowls

On a table in the mart
three 'Willow' pattern bowls nestle
no one's treasure but mine
three for five dollars.

But how deep a pattern goes
feathery tree and Mandarin
a humpback bridge, a sense of terror
and a childhood confusion.

When I was seven I borrowed
a book called *The Willow Pattern Plate*
forgot to return it on time
was sent home to fetch it, crying.

My father thought I meant the plate
and wrapped one from the china cabinet
I carried it close to my heart
all the way back for a second reprimand.

Small wonder my hand in the mart
reached for it: adorable, fatal plate
now turned into three dishes
like little pools of hope.

PIET NIEUWLAND

Paekakariki, At, To, From

The showery southerly knew what it
Was doing when, with Kapiti in classic languid pose
It opened up into a warm hot spring day
As if expecting us.
You've walked this timbered and rock
stacked ocean edge path before,
with echoing Campbell and Baxter,
watched the swells slow heaving roll in
taking a reflected, refracting course up the coast,
waxy green ngaio pulsing with waning spinifex
as sleek Metros glide down and up the argillite fault
line to the piles of Books at Kakariki station.
We take Halcyon and the History
of Temptation for the sweet oncoming days
as another train passes on a camera shutter click,
of Santa bearded O'Leary and his laden shelves.
The rhythm of bass goes on with the Beatles,
New Model Army streaming to the poly-verse beyond
and two gulls ruby red tongued lips charm
with bright gold gazania treasure flowers
this path to fat folios, more station stops
and silvery shape shifting gusts
crossing from Kahurangi
The Sounds

BOB ORR

Seven Haiku

★

i don't care about
frogs
basho's dead

★

so many
stars
to illuminate emptiness

★

after the party
a full moon
and a yellow recycling bin

★

through autumn leaves
the lights
of the city

★

in the backyard
buddha
chopping firewood

★

at daybreak
my coffee pot
remembers south america

*

already spring
sparrows
take out mortgages

SASKIA LEEK

PAINTINGS

1. Untitled, 2014, 390 x 470 mm. Oil on aluminium board.
   Photograph Samuel Hartnett
2. Untitled, 2014, 440 x 540 mm. Oil on aluminium board.
   Photograph Simon Hewson
3. Untitled, 2015, 440 x 540 mm. Oil on aluminium board.
   Photograph Jennifer French from *Necessary Distraction, a painting show*,
   Auckland Art Gallery Toi o Tamaki
4. Untitled, 2015, 440 x 540 mm. Oil on aluminium board.
   Photograph Jennifer French from *Necessary Distraction, a painting show*,
   Auckland Art Gallery Toi o Tamaki
5. Untitled, 2014, 440 x 540 mm. Oil on aluminium board.
   Photograph Samuel Hartnett
6. Untitled, 2015, 440 x 540 mm. Oil on aluminium board.
   Photograph Jennifer French from *Necessary Distraction, a painting show*,
   Auckland Art Gallery Toi o Tamaki
7. Untitled, 2015, 440 x 540 mm. Oil on aluminium board.
   Photograph Simon Cumming
8. Untitled, 2015, 440 x 540 mm. Oil on aluminium board.
   Photograph Simon Cumming

In her recent works, paint is treated as matter, not just a clear pane of glass through which to view the world, although Leek has never been interested in creating easy illusions. Her content becomes a smokescreen; light and colour are central. The audacity of these later images is in their embrace of common subject matter—grapes and autumn leaves recur—alongside jangling juxtapositions of colour. Purple. Orange. Egg-shell blue. These paintings break free of the frame, displaying a boldness not previously apparent. The pathway of Leek's quiet career—from representation, through Cubism and into abstraction—is also the trajectory of 20th-century art.
—Megan Dunn, *New Zealand Listener*, January 2013

Every show I make starts with a period of blankness, having to pull something from the air. It's still very mysterious to me where it comes from ... I'm quite a rummager [in op shops] for faded old fine-art prints ... It's a process of saving and reconfiguring these things, a starting point. I work on them over a period of time and they become something quite different. —Saskia Leek

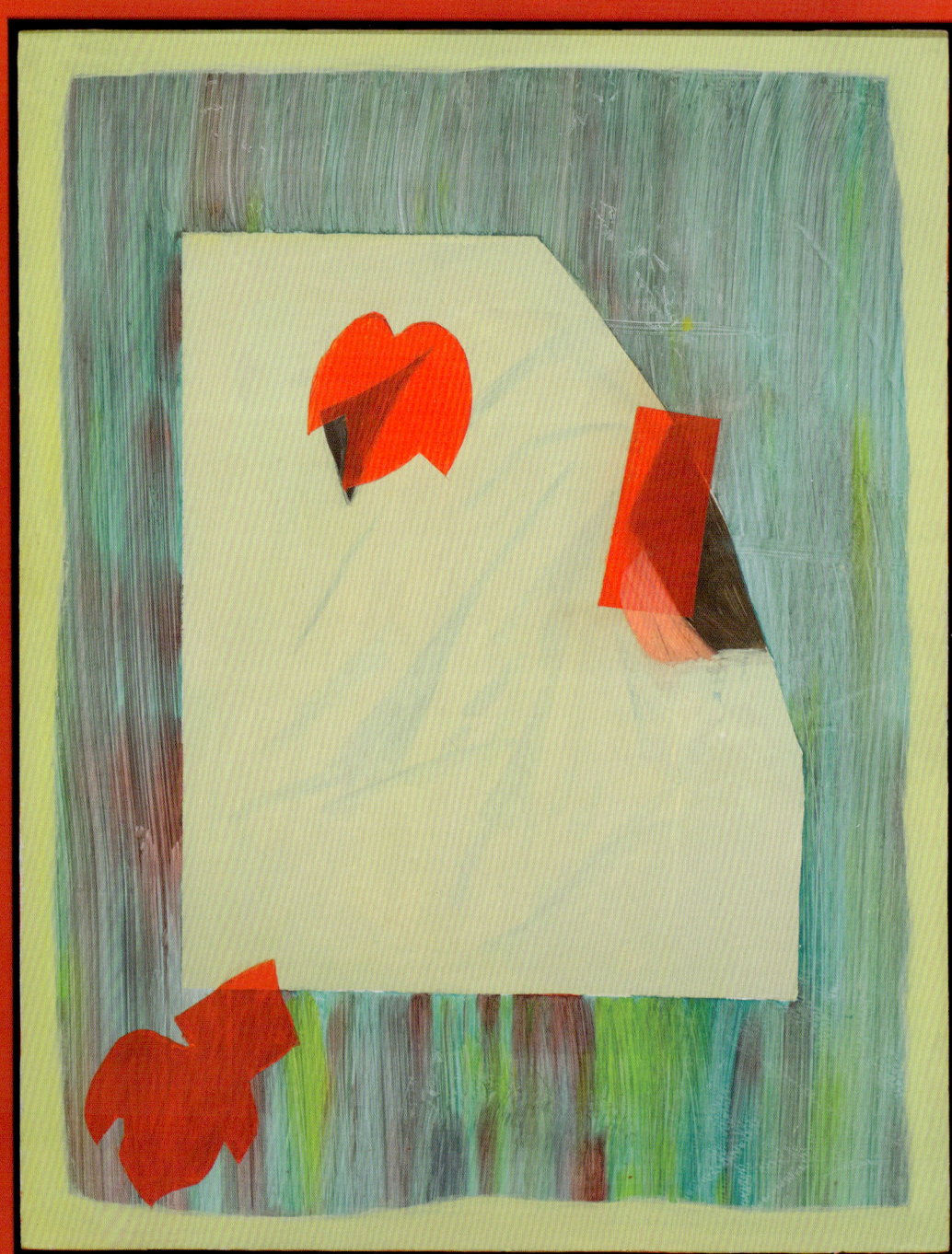

JANET CHARMAN

Yes. Good.

Lana, at all but sixteen, is the youngest of the three McTeague girls. Her mother tells people she was a breech birth and that's what makes her so obstinate. Teachers hearing this at parent interviews have always looked pleasantly back at Mrs McTeague and murmured something noncommittal about Lana's academic future. But this year there was a new dean who got Mr McTeague in too and had a word.

Now Lana has decided to go to The White Ball with Karol Waites.

The Waites are new neighbours, a single mother and her two children. Karol Waites has finished with school and is doing a gap year before he goes away to study, working at Smart Mart by the racecourse. His younger sister Roberta is in the form behind Lana. She dances.

The morning Lana fully makes up her mind about The White Ball, she lies doggo till she hears her dad's truck blat off to the site and then for indescribably longer, until she knows her mum has taken the twins and gone into town to look at ball frocks. Not to buy, just to look.

We'll bring you something back from the French bakery, Lana. What do you want? A pain au chocolat?

Leave her alone, girls.

As soon as the sound of the car engine has subsided away down the road Lana springs out of bed, washes her face, plaits her hair in one braid down her back, puts on her new silver tee and her tiny little red kilt with the rabbit's foot topaz-topped pin; no shoes—she'd only have to take them off to go inside—and stalks out the front gate, around the letterbox and down the next-door driveway. Leading to Karol's place.

It is serious and formal business she has with him so she snakes up the curving concrete steps to his front door and presses the buzzer. Then there is what seems to her, in her nervousness, an awful, lengthy, waiting silence about the house, till finally the ochre hessian curtains at the French windows are swept aside and, all over the living-room floor, courtesy of the little bits of broken mirror in the stuccoed chimneybreast, rainbows scatter.

Hello, Lana. Mrs Waites wrenches at the rather sticking front door. Come in, and she calls along the hall for her daughter. Lana's here, Robbie. She had her ballet exam yesterday. She deserves a sleep-in. It went really well. Madame told us afterwards that the examiner from England said Roberta's technique is exceptional.

No, Mrs Waites, I've come to see Karol. Oh, well, he's still in bed. He's on late shifts at the moment but it's time he was up. Is he expecting you? Heidi Waites moves to the top of the basement steps and yells down to her son. Lana's here to see you, Karol.

Come through to the kitchen, he'll take a minute to surface. Would you like a cup of something? I've just this minute made coffee.

Lana squeezes into the demolition-kauri dining nook in the kitchen. The previous owners inserted this cheek-by-jowl seating into the bay window alcove, where they'd also replaced perfectly good Whitco aluminium windows, which Lana's father managed to rescue and store in his garage, with koru-patterned stained glass.

Lana considers the bitter caramel stench from the percolator rattling and croaking on the smouldering potbelly stove. It's late autumn, quite chilly on mornings like this, but still with some of those long, baking afternoons.

A coffee would be lovely, Mrs Waites. There has to be a first time for everything.

Karol's mother sets a thick white cup before her. There's no handle. The dark arc poured to halfway.

It might be something she won't finish.

Milk, Lana? Sugar? We're a bit behind this morning. Roberta and I didn't get back till after midnight. She's exhausted but we think they'll give her the scholarship.

Heidi Waites swallows some of her coffee and parks a teatowel to dam the kauri-slab benchtop at the point where surface water drips onto the floor. Nothing can upset her today.

Lana's father has always called this house Woodstock. Because the people who lived here before the Waiteses slept their five little kids in together in bunks in the basement—where Karol is now on his own—so the parents could have all the upstairs bedrooms themselves, for yoga and meditation spaces and a study—each.

That family left the district because they wanted their children to go to better schools. When Lana told her parents this was what the neighbours' kids were saying Mr and Mrs McTeague exchanged a look. Better schools? Bullshit. Their landscape architecture business has fallen over because no one in their right mind wants a giant aggregate chess set cluttering up their back yard or a stone frickin' pizza oven.

But then, when the place took so long to sell, Stuart McTeague felt sorry for Russell Falconer and paid him to build one of his handcrafted Tuscan fireboxes next to their pool. Now whenever they stoke it up for a party he always shakes his head and says, Sad guy.

But these new people, these Waiteses, are not at all hippyfied. Actually, people were finding them pretty straightforward. Everyone knows the Falconers' asking price got knocked right down in the end because by the time Heidi Waites came along with the cash they were desperate to cut their losses and get back to the city. She paid the whole lot off in a lump sum from her husband's life insurance. Car accident. She does the accounts at Hydrocorp and is unfailingly polite to everyone, whether or not their cards decline. Which is what you need around here.

Now a pounding of feet up the basement stairs. Karol.

In the doorway with the light from the front room drenching in behind him, he is a triangle of dark torso on long, skinny legs, his face sallow from months of late-night shelf stacking. He's wearing old jeans and his jersey is inside out. A bush of black hair stands up, electric, on the top of his head. Lana is undeterred.

Hi, Karol. Sorry to wake you up. But it's about The White Ball the Soroptomists are having. For the hospice?

No.

At the War Memorial Hall next month. I've come to ask you to take me.

What? I don't want to.

Lana puts her coffee cup down and feels the stupid tears erupt from her head. Karol, a look of puzzlement on his sleep-bleared face, is still in the doorway. Mrs Waites frowns, steps over and whacks him briskly on the arm.

What? He says. I don't want to go.

Then they both stare at Lana who is in the process of scooting herself right around three sides of the kauri table towards the open end of the built-in seat, which will tip her out exactly at the back door. Thank you for the coffee, Mrs Waites, standing now, and smudging away at her eyes with one hand as she tugs at the doorknob with the other.

Stay, Lana, you haven't finished your drink. It's on the deadlock, dear, no one's been out yet. Mrs Waites steps over and turns the deadbolt, releasing her. This time when she wrenches at the handle the door opens and she is able to lurch outside onto the deck and speed down the steps.

As she negotiates their spirals, through the open kitchen window she can hear Mrs Waites tsk tsking over Karol's shaky excuses: But why did she ask me? I hardly know her. I haven't got anything to wear. I can't afford it.

And that's a lie. He's been working full time since last winter. Even if she did expect him to pay for it all—which she wouldn't. No, she would not.

Lana sprints back out the Waiteses' drive and skids around the camellia by their letterbox. Once in her own section she attempts to compose herself. She does not wish ever to discuss this situation again, with anybody.

But just as she reaches the corner of her house Mrs Waites pushes apart the forsythia spears and calls over the boundary pickets: Lana, I'm so sorry. Karol is impossible, so rude!

In her cloak of invisibility, she swishes past Mrs Waites, darts around the recycling bins and lets the pool gate slam behind her. She does not want to hear another word.

Heidi Waites goes back to her kitchen and bangs down the toaster. Karol, I want that awful kitchen table sawn out. Poor Lana. People get trapped behind it. There's barely room to move in here as it is. We shouldn't be jammed in on top of each other whenever visitors come over. And cramped in together every dinnertime. Even with only the three of us—

Mrs Waites, your children need to hear their father's name.

She opens the oven door and it takes a moment to shake the billow of heat from her eyes. Rick would not have put up with this arrangement for five minutes. Oven-gloving the dish of spitting bacon, the fried eggs, now leathery with warming, onto the placemat in the centre of the table. Then she sets the great heap of toast down in front of her stoic child. And sits herself across from him.

Karol, would it kill you to give that little girl a decent night out? You're entitled to a bit of life, son, just like everyone else.

Karol's eyes close. He leans over and pulls the margarine into range, prods the dense yolk of one of the eggs, moves the other two onto his plate. Puts down his knife and fork. Unfolding himself from the bench seat he steps past his mother to the back door, where he hesitates.

I'll take the table and seats out tomorrow afternoon before work. That's if you really want me to. But it will leave a big mess around the walls. And there'll be scars in the floor. Have you thought of that, Mum? He hitches up his jeans and disappears out and down the deck steps.

Heidi Waites pokes her head from the kitchen window in time to see her son wheel around the letterbox into Lana's place. Good job, she says.

Halfway down the McTeagues' driveway, at the crack in the concrete made four years ago when a mate with a crane truck was bringing in the spa pool, Karol stops for a moment.

This is because, unlike Lana, he is not quite sure which door he ought to knock at. But then he heads towards the back of the house, unlatches the pool gate, bounds onto the verandah and raps sharply at the half-open ranchslider. No one responds but then he sees Lana reflected in the glass. She is behind him, stretched out on a sunbed beside the pool.

Her arms are crossed over her chest and she's texting. Karol turns from the reflection and half waves. She seems oblivious. He walks down onto the lawn and along the poolside to where his shadow covers her legs and she looks up. Her face is blotchy. She has changed into faded black bike pants, or perhaps they were already on under the kilt. And her breasts, underneath a loose grey athletics singlet, are drawn up in some stringy kind of red halter. Behind him the water glints. Lana is dry.

We barely know each other, he says.

She throws down her phone, scrambles to her feet.

Anyway you're too young to go out with me—I'm eighteen, he adds.

A funny little hiss comes out of her chest. Then Lana thrusts out both her arms and in one abrupt jerk, pushes him backwards into the pool.

She stands above him, watching him heave and gasp. He sinks twice before she realises. And lets herself down over the side. Tries to evade his walloping arms as she paddles around behind him, where she lands her own sharp whack on the side of his head. It's only then that he can hear her shouting: 'Don't, Karol! Don't fight me. Relax'. Somehow, from behind him, her hand is cupped under his chin. I've got you. I'll get you to the shallow end for God's sake Karol I'm helping you.

The water stops surging around them and he can feel her tugging him bit by bit in the endless strokes it takes to get to where he won't be in over his head. Stand up, she says. Stand up.

His denims are icy, plastered against his legs, weighing down the lower part of his body. But he finds he is able to bend over now and cough and splutter and smooth the wetness from his face and dripping hair. He looks up to see that Lana has a wide red welt across half her face where one of his floundering arms must have caught her. He passes his hand over the smack she gave him.

She's heaving sobs. You egg, she says, you could have drowned us both. But Karol bares his teeth at her in a snarl of a smile. He turns and wades straight across the shallow part towards the ladder. As he goes forward he palms the water aside in two deep repeating curves which speed from his body as he strides and then he's clambered up, even leaning down to try to give her a hand when she follows him to the side. This she grimly refuses. Bouncing herself: one two UP and out of the water in a single expert thrust. Then they're standing face to face on the tiled surround, their clothes streaming.

Karol thinks of something he would like to say: This is the most surprising moment of my life. But Lana has turned away and is pulling a stack of towels off the shelf under the oven. She tucks one around herself and drops back down on the pool chaise with a kind of sulky finality.

He wraps a towel around his own waist. Pulls his saturated jersey off over his head, drapes a second towel across his bare shoulders.

Lana has crumpled herself up at the top end of the lounger. He turns away from her and, inside the smother of fabric fastened around his middle, starts to shuck off his jeans. Silently she watches him complete these awkwardly modest contortions. The pants kicked into a heap, the towel tightened.

Everyone knows about you, Karol, she says. Like an old man he lowers himself onto the lounger's footrest. Those boys who met up with you at Rydges Hut, they've told everyone.

He's shivering and he starts to cough again. His stomach makes a singing gurgle and he presses his hands over it. Lana gets up and pulls a picnic blanket off the shelf, holds it out to him. I'm sorry, she says. I shouldn't have pushed you.

He throws the sodden towel off his shoulders and huddles the blanket's woolliness around himself. A paperback she had been reading is open in the grass by his foot. Karol toes it closed and reaches across to pick it up. *Art of the Renaissance*. He leafs through it for a moment. Venus Aphrodite. Adam and Eve expelled. The Crucifixion. Stuffed with biblical paintings, but is there any true faith in these arty types who write about them? He carefully slides the book onto the oven benchtop.

When's your exam?

I don't believe in exams. They're bullshit.

But you believe the bull you've heard about me, Lana. Be honest. That's why you asked me.

It's no big deal, Karol. We'd just be there as friends. Everyone's going. My sisters have got tickets. But Dad says I'm too young even though they're only a year older than me. So I'm going too. I thought if it was you who invited me, he'd change his mind.

Because you've heard I'm sick and dying.

Mum and Dad will agree if this is your last and only chance.

I'm not sick, Lana. I don't go out much because I'm saving up to go to Bible College. I've already saved four thousand dollars, which is enough to enrol in the Mission Programme at Destination U.

You don't have to bullshit me, Karol. I know what you've got, everyone does.

Karol sits up straight, arms crossed at his waist. But do you know what else, Lana? God keeps me safe. He always has. And your mates who talk about me are in thrall to Satan. I knew they were working themselves up to do something to me. Something you don't want to know. But I had to stay there with them because the weather was too bad to leave the hut. They counted on that. So I told them I was ill.

He takes a rough breath and shrugs off the blanket, pushes down the towel at his waist. I said I was infectious. There, on the silk of his belly, just across from his hipbone, is a pout of red flesh. For a little way around it the skin is stained. Like coffee. Karol looks down at himself. It's an ileostomy. I mostly have to keep a bag stuck over it. For the waste, he says. He wraps himself into the blanket again. When I was a baby in Indonesia, I got amoebic dysentery. My dad had engineering work up there. They did this operation to save my life.

The boys say you've got cancer.

It's a stoma, but I told them it was a tumour so they'd leave me alone. After they saw it they were afraid to touch me.

Why didn't you report them if they tried to do something to you? Did you tell your mum?

Do you want people to look at me as even more of a freak? No one would believe me anyway. Your boys are so full of themselves, Lana. You don't want to believe me, do you?

They're not my boys.

Well I just want to forget about it and leave. My mother wants everything to be normal for our family. Anyway, the reason I can't go to the ball with you is nothing to do with that. I already have a girlfriend and we're unofficially engaged. We're both going to Bible College in July. We met over Easter, at camp. We're getting married after graduation and we're going to work overseas in the missions. She's saving up too.

Lana says nothing.

Also I don't dance, he says. And there will be drinking at the ball which is a sin. Those boys who tried it on were all drunk. But maybe not as drunk as they were acting since they sure left me alone when they thought they might catch something. I knew they'd told people from the way the women at work were suddenly so nice to me. Always asking me how I am and using the hand sanitiser if they accidentally touch me. I'm surprised you're willing to be seen with me.

Lana's fingers are tap tapping her cheek. I think I'm getting a black eye. She looks at her reflection on her phone. The skin above her cheek is already darkening. What am I going to tell them? Dad will go mad.

Why don't you say that when I came over here to very politely explain that I can't take you to the ball, you pushed me in the pool? Why don't we tell them that?

Okay, but then we'd better add that after I jumped in to save your life, you went psycho and tried to kill me.

By mistake, he says.

You're eighteen years old, Karol. You can drive and vote, why the hell can't you swim?

The bag.

But … you're not wearing one.

I don't have to until after I eat. He twists around to look at the pool. It felt good in there once I knew I was going to live. My dad loved swimming but they couldn't get me to try it when I was little. I suppose I knew everyone would stare. They never forced me. Dad was embarrassed.

I could teach you—I've been swimming my whole life.

Yeah? He presses his hand over the place on the towel, at the little spout.

You'll have to hire a suit, she says.

No, I can buy a waterproof appliance; I saw one in a catalogue. It'd only take a few days to get here. He trails his fingers into the chill and then swings his legs over the poolside. I'll wear something tight, to keep it in place. Maybe bike pants.

Yes, she says. Good.

Her mum has some concealer, and by then the marks should have faded.

The spinal knots unreel down his back. They look like something she could draw.

WILL LEADBEATER

Three Variations on 'The Red Wheelbarrow' by William Carlos Williams

1.
Don't always
rely on others
to carry your load:

push your own barrow—
and it doesn't
have to be red
or glazed with rainwater

and you can forget about
the white chickens.

2.
Nothing depends upon
a green wheelbarrow

spattered with
white plum petals

for it doesn't
have a wheel

and the white chickens
have all grown up
and flown the coop.

3.
Everything depends
upon a white wheelbarrow
spattered with dried bloodstains,
for it will be presented
in the courtroom
as 'Exhibit A'.

VIVIENNE PLUMB

Matters of Accommodation

Then I realise there could be a problem
with finding a place to live in Christchurch,
after heaps of phoning I manage to get
a room with a tiny bathroom and a bed,
the kitchen is communal, at the end
of the corridor. I take this room sight unseen
and am required to sign a tenancy
agreement with the landlord and to pay ten
weeks rent in advance, plus bond. People say
to me they have a relative in Christchurch
who wants to 'get out', as if it is some kind
of prison on an island named Nowhere.

A Christchurch friend tells me she and her husband
are paying eight hundred dollars a week rent
for a three-bedroom villa, although it's
the insurance company who pays this fee
while my friends' damaged red-zone area
house is being repaired.

Now this won't hurt at all, I imagined
they said, and in a moment I was uplifted
and transported to Christchurch.
Thick white dust everywhere.
Dust and crap in the air and some say also
poisonous particles, like asbestos,
or concrete dust. Christchurch offers the same thing
wherever I go: dust and scones.

Coming out of the shopping centre I can
see a walker frame and a pair of feet sticking
out of the bus shelter. Shirley is on her
way to the crematorium, something about
flowers for the deceased sister of someone
she knew as a child. I live in the rest home
now, she says, I have to be back for tea by five.
Shirley knows everything possible
about the Metro buses and tells me where
I need to go to purchase the bus card.

The relentless noisy humming of my 'bar-size'
refrigerator cancels out the snores
of the next-room neighbour, PhD student
in engineering, who wakes at one each morning
to skype his wife and children in Sri Lanka;
the wall between our rooms is thinner than I'd
thought.

Two plump Malaysian women are sharing
the room situated next to the communal
kitchen. They are studying engineering
but when they cook they fill the kitchen with black
smoke. Abdus, Akmals, Omars, Huafangs and Kims
and Angelitos, the uncollected mail
in the lounge says it all. In the kitchen
you can see the oily pans and the empty
rice cookers, and you can feel them in their rooms
late at night: sweating, huddled over their
laptops, skyping Sri Lanka, praying, dreaming.

Signs of violence at the local bus stop
shelter where a man was sleeping during the
warmer months. An entire glass wall of the shelter

has been smashed. Who knows what happened?
There are plenty of angry people in Christchurch.

Every shed, every garage, anything
vaguely occupiable has someone
in it. While the weather holds some sleep in tents
and others are in cars and vans.

Shipping containers have been used for so
many things in Christchurch, from storage to small
shops, now the Christchurch Press reports that they will
be transformed into thirteen 'studio-size pods'
(no windows), rentable for three hundred dollars
a week. Not be outdone, the Inland Revenue
is reminding everyone they must pay tax
on any rental even if it's just your
old caravan.

The fire door opposite my room slams shut
again. A smell of toast, never a smell of roast.
In the communal kitchen a handwritten
sign pleads Could you please wipe the bench of any
surface water. The largest refrigerator
(on its last legs) makes its usual gulping
sound. Please keep the kitchen clean and homely.
Something smelly (and very unattended)
is simmering on the stove.

Back to the minuses, says the elderly
Christchurch checkout operator serving me
in the supermarket. She'd know. The frost
has coated the world blue and it is minus
four outside.
If you are a walker, the city has become
a barren endless stretch of muddy broken

footpaths, carparks and car yards.
They call it a 'donut' city meaning
nothing in the middle, but there's a shifting
horizon: bulldozed flat one month and then
the next month the fragile skeleton structure
of something new and shiny begins to protrude.

Outside the Linwood Eastgate Mall a young man
begins to talk to me. His trackie pants
are pulled high above his waist and he has
a key hanging on a cord around his neck.
Suddenly, a totally empty bus comes
screeching to a halt. Its destination
head sign on the front shows the words *Special
Events*, and the young man springs aboard
immediately, swipes his card,
and the bus roars away. He was the only
passenger.

Aah, the mysteries of this southern city.
Farewell, Christchurch. I have to let it all go,
let it bleed out of my ears, my eyes, my nose.
Was that merely a distant worrying dream?
No.
I board my own *Special Events* plane and fly out.

I.K. PATERSON-HARKNESS

Middlemarch

I sit atop the disused train in Middlemarch as night
switches blue dusk clear for colourless dim,
and deliberate on whether I want to be your wife.

The rusted steel is warm and softer
than the brown grass burnt stiff by the reckless summer,
snapping under the paws of a foraging rabbit.

The kids are in the park sleeping damply in their cabin.
I left you in the communal lounge sucking back
a Speights Old Dark with the Spanish cycling couple,

Talking about trains and steam.
Parallel lines leading us headlong into the future.
Parallel lines carrying us over hills and over canyons.

The lady in Ranfurly who ran the info station
showed us to the room out back,
scarcely lit but for the grey tones of flickering footage

Of a crowd of locals and hopefuls and farmers
waving hats and handkerchiefs as the first train left Clyde,
and imagining that the line would last.

Soon after we married we drove a van to Roxburgh
and parked up by the lake,
and drank a cask of something red and terrible,

And I nearly pissed myself when you told me you used to
dance to Mariah Carey, naked, while your parents watched the news,
and I warned you to never stop talking.

Driving today across the rock-strewn plains from Alex,
the kids dripping ice blocks and kicking in the back,
I swore if you mentioned the hills again I'd kill you.

Then you said,
'God, take a look at these hills, won't you?
The shadows move and change with the sun.
One bright field is soon sliced through darkness, yet
One dark gully is now a river of light.'
And I said, 'You're right. Nothing stays the same.'

The roosting birds don't notice me sitting here,
silently absorbing the warm depths of Middlemarch,
too burnt out to move from this motionless train.

ELIZABETH WELSH

Her Mountain Parents Meeting

They think they remember bathing together naked in the cloak of a gorge
    spring floe.
They think. (tops, access corridors, breath hurting on a polar barren dawn)

she charted splayed structures of the podocarp broadleaved forest and the
Cangiante viridian-yellow of the alpine herbfields; he took care of the braided
rivers wending gracefully to the harried foot of glaciers, heaving wetland
swamps;
   ache, ache, make, forsake, ache, partake, make

It's hard to know how to be   with a mother who is a mountain
It's hard to feel how to be   with a father who is a mountain

to understand that luminous bond;
that bewilderingly stretched distance

ROBERT MCLEAN

A View of the Canterbury Plains

i.m. Colin McCahon

We owe our provenance to that hand
    and those long-sighted eyes
that limned the boundary of the flat land
    from which the hills must rise.

Across those hills he scrawled a text
    cribbed from Jeremiah
of what had been and would come next
    in characters of fire.

The hills balked at the rowdy script
    that smirched their subtle flanks;
the flat land, though, remained tight lipped—
    for which the hills gave thanks.

Anachronism never pleases.
    The erstwhile prophet glowered
and painted little baby Jesus
    colicky in a cowshed.

The landscape gasped and turned its back
    on such a silly slight.
And all at once, its patent lack
    of people came to light.

So silence filled the empty space—
    belittled for his starkness,

    the painter drained the cup of grace
        and fell back into darkness.

And all the while, the slow landscape
    bided its time. It's born and dies
time and again, for no man's sake,
    from which the hills must rise.

MARY MACPHERSON

Inward

(Janet Paul exhibition, Alexander Turnbull Library gallery, 2014)

The small room quivers
with the scissored blue knowledge
of your eyes, kindly
dragging the scene askew—coffeepot,
cows and lipstick flowers
teeter. The poet called it *god speaking
through us* your fast river
of celebratory decoration, land,
and eyes reflecting inward.
In seconds, breathing moistly on the glass—
lives on our backs, property elsewhere—
we riffle through jewels,
our turbulence inchoate

BILL DIREEN

An Extract from Work in Progress

I was walking backwards into night,
gaze fixed on the interior,
a pulsing pumping green light expanding
as if at the points of a compass
or the minute marks of a clock.

No terror behind,
and the moon full and white as snow,
only this glow uneasy unnatural,
glow that continues
when another light has been extinguished,
an underlight in a darkness
that is our presence.

I do not seek another
another land another wife,
companion or child,
nor resent this daily task
to remain silent and record
words that will not offend.

You couldn't have measured the light
it was so brilliant;
it was the wheel itself
burning labour disintegrating my heart;
the song had outsung the singer.

Day had returned
to a continent calling
to tomorrow,
cold crisp and the moon fierce;
such light generating so little heat;
constellations beating quietly;
driven, the two,
the large and small stars,
behind that massive range.

Firemen in orange overalls,
behind them the pub
where you manage to live with your injuries.

And these water-words
one must not touch them—
once they've been laid down
they are the marriage of morning.

RON RIDDELL

St Paul's Standing

The blood yet stirring in my veins
the towers of St Paul's still standing

sitting there in the gathering dusk
an ageing pilgrim at evensong

wearing glasses, a dark suit
a certain air of refinement

which in the circumstances
does not count for much

yet when the incense is lit
I'm moved to ask the question

'You're not T.S. Eliot, are you?'
'What if I am?' he replies.

'I thought … I thought you were
you were once the leading light …'

he glanced at me a second or so
and turned his eyes away

looking up I saw his gaze
steady, sure, upon the altar

as he stroked the wooden rail
atop the polished pew

'What are you doing here?' I asked
'Pleading for my daily bread

as my blood still stirs—and you?'
yet no celebrant arrived

though we waited until midnight
though we waited until dawn

we waited down the silences
the enchantments and deceits

we waited down the tumult
of ceaseless lives and deaths

we waited down, we waited late
until we could wait no more

until I saw in my delirium
were my eyes now playing tricks?

it seemed I caught his gaze
what was it—did he steal a wink?

a one-in-a-million
once-in-a-lifetime, throwaway-line:

'yes, we are the thousand-and-one
you have been nightly seeking'

then he gets up and slowly walks away
I throw my hands up, act despair

'what did we know, what did we share
what brought us here and made us one

from Clerkenwell to Cerro Nutibara
one brown river that just keeps rolling?'

he does not turn, which is no surprise
the air whispers back a part reply

the air which circles vulture-dark
above the teeming towers and shanties

while we are blinded in the ruins
of steady rain and ebb-flow of the tide

while the blood still stirs within
bright flags of hope without unfolding.

The Boat Man

for Bob Orr

You don't say much but when you do
the words are apt; well tempered—

rising, falling; waves on the dark swell
surging in, giving off faint flicks of light.

You don't say much but when you do
you make them count—the words fall

fecund from your lip, quickened
by salt spray; the lustre of sea

the loom of wide horizons; charted
yet—how's this?—you, a navigator

in such seas would forge new frontiers
thresholds of sense & sensibility.

The eye's twinkling holds fast and true—
there's that beacon yet, that reflection

of leading light, that makes way
for vessels homing in 'mid sounds of

gulls, horns & sailors' larrikining:
the smiling light returns to roost

the Ithaca light sailing sweet to port
to chants and cries, *Who's this? Who's this?*

Yet you do not put off your course
of scant-surmise-and-straight-purpose.

No game here but the bell ringing clear
in the bright autumnal breathing.

Who says you're not the gambling type?
I've seen you work the deck with hands

wind-torn and worn by rucking storms
that would wreck the best of grinders.

Boatman, hold your form; stay true
to your hand and the hands that hold you.

See how the wind drops; let the waves
coast you in, you and your *Calypso* crewmen.

VICTOR RODGER

From *Skip to the End*

After their first fuck, the man took a thick silver ring off his almost-black finger and offered it to Robert.

'Take this as a symbol of my love.'

His Samoan accent was strong so his s's came out as sh's. *Thish. Ash. Shymbol.*

Robert, even though he'd never admit it, was inclined to dismiss him as just another hot Fob full of cheesy one-liners. But the ring—the ring was interesting, even if the sex had been unspectacular. (As Robert fucked the man, his moans had climbed higher and higher until they almost hit a feminine register. When he fucked, he liked his men to grunt in a basso profundo—never higher than an alto.)

Robert took the ring and held it in his hand. Heavy. Definitely not cheap. He slid it onto his just-olive finger and admired it.

'Maybe one day, you and me, we get married?' *Tay. Ket.*

The man raised his eyebrows twice in quick succession.

Robert smiled.

If only he could remember the man's name.

'Thanks, man.'

For now, that would have to do.

After their second fuck (much better than the first, since the man kept his grunting low), the man opened the wardrobe in his small Manurewa bedroom and pulled out three boxes. He placed them on the bed.

'Have a look.' *Haff.*

Robert opened the first box: inside were two beautifully hand-stitched black leather shoes.

'They're beautiful,' he said, both surprised and excited. His heart began to race as he checked the size.

'Twelves.' The magical number.

The other boxes contained the exact same shoes in tan and chocolate.

'Take them,' the man said, looking at Robert fondly.

The shoes were beautiful—more beautiful than any Robert possessed. Certainly more beautiful than his tatty brown dress shoes which lay underneath his quickly discarded pants and t-shirt.

'You don't want them?'

The man shrugged. 'Too big.'

There was the question as to why the man had three identical pairs of expensive shoes that were too big for him—but Robert didn't care. Instead, he grabbed a sock from the floor, put it on his foot and tried to slide his foot inside one of the shoes.

But no matter how hard he tried, his foot resisted. Robert silently cursed his Samoan father for the one thing he'd ever given him: wide feet.

The man stood there, naked and amused as Robert desperately tried to get his foot inside the shoe.

'Like Cinderella,' the man said. *Shindarella*.

Robert grimaced. He had absolutely no intention of being an Ugly Sister. He pushed and pushed, willing his foot into the shoe. It was a battle he'd fought many times, around the world, with his wide, flat feet. Sometimes he'd won; sometimes he'd lost. But this time, he was absolutely determined to get his foot inside.

The man seemed confused by Robert's determination: 'Too small, uh?'

Robert's natural impulse was to glare at the man but instead he kept pushing. And pushing. And pushing, willing the leather to give a little more each time.

Finally, when sweat was trickling down his temples, Robert's foot slid into the shoe. His foot felt like it had been placed into an ever-tightening vice—but it was in.

He grabbed another sock, forced the other shoe on and then stood naked, his little toes throbbing. He gingerly walked towards a full-length mirror.

'Sole—you sure they fit okay?'

The shoes were killing him. Every step was absolute agony. But Robert was determined his wide feet would eventually make the shoes succumb to his width. It would just take time: time and persistence.

Robert looked up at the man. Fuck. He still couldn't remember his name.

'Thanks, man.'

For a moment he wondered what the man might bestow on him if they fucked for a third time but he looked at his watch: it was time to go.

Robert got dressed and hobbled out of the man's house with the three shoeboxes under his arms.

The man looked at him, clearly concerned at the way he was walking.

'Sole—you sure you okay?'

Robert nodded and smiled.

'Sweet. For real.'

They drove in silence: the man had agreed to drop Robert at his friend Patsy's house.

The man rested one hand on Robert's thigh, slowly stroking it up and down as he drove down Weymouth Road. Among the people-movers sagging with sticky-fingered children and arguing parents, Robert was surprised that the man clearly held no fear about being seen being affectionate with another man.

Robert looked over at him. He had a strong profile. Impossibly smooth skin. Beautiful full lips. Fine jet-black hair. It was obvious why Robert had drunkenly made a beeline for him at the club last night. And for a fleeting moment he wondered how his mother had felt, meeting his father, fresh from Samoa, for the first time.

The man was about to pull into Patsy's driveway but Robert had no intention of being seen with him in public and instructed him to pull over to the side of the road.

Robert got out of the car, his feet pulsating as though each toe had been hit with a hammer.

The man winked at him. 'Vili mai.'

Robert frowned: his Samoan barely went beyond pleasantries and swearwords.

The man clarified: 'Call me.'

Robert noticed Patsy in the distance, watching with interest from the deck of her dilapidated house, her short, stout frame encased in a faded white bathrobe, her skin a dark chocolate against it.

'Fa,' he said, quickly.

'Ia, fa.'

Robert watched as the man drove away, then turned to face Patsy, who had one plucked, bemused eyebrow arched.

'O ai le la kama?'

Robert ran through the phrases he recognised in his head, trying to translate without having to ask: Kama—*man*. O ai. *Who?* She was asking who the man was?

'Just a friend.'

'A friennnnnnnnd?' The word in Patsy's mouth was thick with derision. Her eyes looked at the new shoes and the shoeboxes under Robert's arms.

'You been shopping?

'Kinda.'

Patsy shook her head: 'Oi sole.'

It was not quite dusk. Inside the house Robert could hear Patsy's husband, Napz, reprimanding one of their children and a child's stifled cries.

Robert took two geisha-girl steps towards the house, his little toes pulsating prisoners desperate to break free from their jail.

Patsy clicked her tongue against the roof of her mouth as she watched him: 'E, kalofae si Little Mermaid.'

Robert was about to follow her inside when she looked down at his shoes. He knew she meant for him to take them off before entering the house.

'Come on, Pats. If you'd seen how long it took to get them on …'

Pats raised one eyebrow.

'But …'

Patsy raised the other eyebrow.

Robert sighed, and then with great effort and even greater reluctance, kicked his shoes off.

Ahhhhh, the sweet, sweet release …

He looked down at the other discarded shoes outside the front door: well-worn jandals, grubby sneakers, scuffed black church shoes.

'Are they safe out here?'

'Ki`o,' Patsy said as she moved inside.

Robert couldn't bear the thought of them being nicked. He balanced the three shoeboxes under one arm, then bent down to pick up his beautiful new shoes.

'I'll bring them inside. Just in case.'

The Landfall Review

Landfall Review Online

www.landfallreview.com

Reviews posted since October 2015
(Reviewer's name in brackets)

October 2015

Jim Allen: The skin of years, Philip Dadson & Tony Green with Jim Allen (Jonathon Marshall)
The Mermaid Boy, John Summers (Denis Harold)
The Hiding Places, Catherine Robertson (Helen Watson White)
Autobiography of a Marguerite, Zarah Butcher-McGunnigle (Alice Miller)
Trouble, Jenny Powell (Alice Miller)
There are No Horses in Heaven, Frankie McMillan (Alice Miller)
Heke-nuku-mai-nga-iwi Busby: Not Here by Chance, Jeff Evans (Gerry Te Kapa Coates)
Vertical Living: The architectural centre and the remaking of Wellington, Julia Gatley & Paul Walker (David Eggleton)
Shigeru Ban: Cardboard cathedral, Andrew Barrie (David Eggleton)
Bungalow: From heritage to contemporary, Nicola Stock (David Eggleton)
Marae: Te Tatau Pounamu, Muru Walters, Robin Walters & Sam Walters (David Eggleton)
Beyond the State, Bill McKay & Andrea Stevens (David Eggleton)
Down the Long Driveway You'll See It, Mary Gaudin & Matthew Arnold (David Eggleton)

November 2015

A Place to Go On From: The Collected Poems of Iain Lonie, David Howard (ed) (Lawrence Jones)
Some of Us Eat the Seeds, Morgan Bach (Robert McLean)
The Glass Rooster, Janis Freegard (Robert McLean)
Jerusalem Sonnets, Love, Wellington Zoo, David Beach (Robert McLean)
Atonement, Vaughan Rapatahana (Robert McLean)
Breath Dances, Peter Bland (Pat White)
Bones in the Octagon, Carolyn McCurdie (Pat White)
The Invisible Mile, David Coventry (Brian Clearkin)
No Relation, Thomas Pors Koed (Ted Jenner)
F4: In the Interval, Susan Jowsey, Marcus Williams, Jesse Williams & Mercy Williams (Max Oettli)
An Urban Quest for Chlorophyll, Jennifer Gilliam & Dieneke Jansen (Max Oettli)

December 2015

Maurice Gee: Life and Work, Rachel Barrowman (Patricia McLean)
The Lives of Colonial Objects, Annabel Cooper, Lachy Paterson & Angela Wanhalla (eds) (Edmund Bohan)
Chappy, Patricia Grace (Simone Oettli)
An Imitation of Life, Laura Solomon (Raewyn Alexander)
Hello Boys and Girls! – A New Zealand Toy Story, David Veart (Nicholas Reid)
View from the Road, Arno Gasteiger (David Eggleton)
Te Atatu Me: Photographs of an urban New Zealand village, John B. Turner (David Eggleton)
Meet Me in the Square: Christchurch 1983–1987, David Cook (David Eggleton)
Frozen, Peter Black (David Eggleton)
Creamy Psychology: Photographs by Yvonne Todd (David Eggleton)
See What I Can See: New Zealand photography for the young and curious, Gregory O'Brien (David Eggleton)

February 2016

Being Here: Selected poems, Vincent O'Sullivan (Mark Houlahan)
Thuds Underneath, Brent Kininmont (Piet Nieuwland)
Native Bird, Bryan Walpert (Piet Nieuwland)
Generation Kitchen, Richard Reeve (Piet Nieuwland)
The Predictions, Bianca Zander (Nicholas Reid)
Infidelities, Kirsty Gunn (Tasha Haines)
Hold My Teeth While I Teach You to Dance, Mike Johnson (Michael O'Leary)
Fallout: A Tito Ihaka Novel, Paul Thomas (Jennifer Lawn)

March 2016

Beyond Puketapu, Dunstan Ward (Denys Trussell)
Shaggy Magpie Songs, Murray Edmond (Denys Trussell)
Looking Out To Sea, Kevin Ireland (Denys Trussell)
Kūpapa: The Bitter Legacy of Māori Alliances with the Crown, Ron Crosbie (Gerry Te Papa Coates)
The Blinding Walk, K.M. Ross (Richard Taylor)
The Party Line, Sue Orr (Christine Johnston)
Landfall, Tim Jones (Michelle Elvy)
The Dharma Punks, Ant Sang (Melinda Johnston)
Sam Zabel and the Magic Pen, Dylan Horrocks (Melinda Johnston)

FICTION

Possession
by Andrew Dean

The Back of His Head, by Patrick Evans (Victoria University Press, 2015), 374pp, $30

Mark Williams began his review of *Gifted*, Patrick Evans' 2010 novel about Janet Frame and Frank Sargeson—a novel published when I was Evans' student at the University of Canterbury—by admitting that he was 'sceptical' about a 'curious rumour' going around literary circles at the time. Williams had heard that Evans 'had done something exceptionally good', but, having read one of Evans' earlier novels, *Making It* (1989), he found such a rumour hard to believe, as he still 'struggled to expel from consciousness the conversation it contains between the central character and his penis'. It was with some surprise that he reported that *Gifted* was, in fact, a very good work (even if it may be simply 'the one first-rate novel we are all supposed to contain').

The phallologue that occupies the beginning of Williams' review is not out of place in Patrick Evans' work, neither in his fiction nor in his literary criticism. Charles Brasch's penis is the subject of particular attention in Evans' writing, such as in an essay he published in *Landfall* 212 in 2006, 'New Zealand's missing penis'. Recounting the episode in which Brasch found that his 'cup, so to speak, ran over', after the man with whom he was infatuated, Harry Scott, returned home, Evans finds evidence of a larger story within New Zealand literature, what he describes as the 'abstract and symbolically patriarchal phallus' of colonialism. In his most recent book of criticism, *The Long Forgetting*, he begins one of his chapters by citing an article published in the *Listener*, which revealed that actor Peter Varley may have seduced Barry Crump, the author of novels such as *A Good Keen Man* and *Hang on a Minute, Mate*. The article clearly tickles Evans' fancy and he draws from it with glee. He has Crump going off to the bedroom asking his soon-to-be-lover, 'You will be gentle, won't you, Peter?' 'After the latter's query at the moment of conjunction ("Am I hurting you, Barry?"), Evans writes, Crump replied, 'Nup. She's beaut.'

Over the course of Evans' career he has, without doubt, been one of our most provocative critics and writers—and I mean that in both senses. He is best known for his criticism on Janet Frame, work which one feminist critic said has led her over the years to both 'delight' and 'despair'. His unauthorised biographical criticism on Frame, which makes up the first two chapters of his 1977 scholarly monograph on her work, drew Frame's ire to such an extent that she wrote to him soon afterward, calling him a 'Porlock Person'. Evans added fuel to the fire in his 1993 article 'The case of the disappearing author', by recounting how he became in his early years 'a sort of critical *paparazzo* … always trying for that special, authentic shot as I stumble through the shrubbery of her life'. The mill of controversy kept on turning: after the publication of Michael King's 2000 biography, *Wrestling with the Angel: A life of Janet Frame*, a book that was meant to put an end to the endless speculation about the author's life, Evans said the biographer had done little more than sit 'on Frame's knee as she herself once sat on the knee of her favourite teacher', becoming her 'ventriloquist's dummy'. Hostile responses to *Gifted*, especially the 2013 play based on the book, ended up in the newspapers.

Despite all of this (and perhaps because of it) Evans has been one of the pre-eminent critics of Frame's work and of New Zealand literature in general over the past few decades. He has forced a reckoning with our literary culture and explored territory made taboo for personal, political, historical or theoretical reasons. In his latest novel, *The Back of His Head* (2015), he takes on this culture and these problems in what I would suggest is his best, and darkest, work yet.

The Back of His Head tells the story of the later years of a Nobel Prize-winning writer from Christchurch, Raymond Lawrence, and of the literary hangers-on who find themselves attached to him. Lawrence's writing itself is only glimpsed for the briefest of moments, at the beginning and at the end. The novel is instead primarily told in the voices of two narrators, his nephew and adopted son, Peter Orr, and Lawrence's carer during his lengthy decline, Thom Ham.

Orr, writing some years after the death of the author, is now in charge of his uncle's literary estate. His job is to keep the writer's memory alive, which he does through running tours of the 'Residence' (tours that attract fewer and fewer visitors each year) and handling permissions for copyright and quotation (also reducing in number). As 'Keeper of the Flame' he also handles the Raymond Lawrence Trust's finances, which are in precipitous decline—in one particularly testy meeting the trustees discuss selling furniture from the Residence to help fund necessary maintenance.

Lawrence's carer, Ham, is a weightlifter, an ordinary Kiwi bloke who lives at some remove from Orr and the culturesphere. In between sessions in the gym, Ham spends much of the novel lifting Lawrence up, putting him down, getting him going, and then, later, trying to make him stop. We hear his voice from the tapes recorded by a biographer, only ever identified as 'Patrick', who is paying for information about Lawrence.

The author's ghost haunts the Residence and the trustees' lives. Orr finds himself in the Residence late at night, calling for the spirit of Lawrence to emerge out of the carefully preserved carpets and wall furnishings, in the hope that he still might be there. He writes that it is 'as if I'm listening to someone else who's inside me and who shouldn't be there, who shouldn't be'. Lawrence haunts another of the trustees, Robert Semple, too. Semple tells Orr the great author destroyed him 'as a poet and as a human being', alongside doing 'exactly the opposite'. He would have achieved nothing 'if the Master hadn't taken him there', he says. Orr's own experience runs much deeper, though. For him, Lawrence is, quite simply, 'the Master':

> He transformed everything he touched, everyone he touched. I knew to let him do it, because he was who he was. Some people make their own rules, and others are there to obey them. That's just how it is. One submits to the greater force. One submits to a force of nature.

Orr recalls his young adult life with the author. In a scene of shocking brutality, he remembers when Lawrence threatened to 'write' on him with a knife—'stay *still*, stay *still*—no, don't *move*, fuck you'. In another memory he recalls Lawrence standing over him, threatening him by running his hand along his nephew's spine: 'There's a nerve in a man's back,' Lawrence says to the teenaged Orr. 'If you find it you can paralyse him.'

Each of the trustees has their own story of Lawrence's sadism, stories that to them represent moments of great intimacy. 'There slowly evolved between us what I came to think of as a *lash of love*,' Orr writes. 'I don't think I've ever been so *close* to anyone in those moments when, somehow, I got something right.'

The Lawrence who has entered public memory is much less troubling, of course, and the comedy of the book arises out of the disjunction between the author we come to know from Orr and Ham and the author that the public wishes existed. The executors are forever finding more evidence of the author's malfeasance and by the end Evans has them dumping Lawrence's manuscripts into a fire in order to 'safeguard … the Master's name'.

Lawrence's later life did not help the trust's task: after he had entered the literary stratosphere he spent his time attempting to wreck his own memory. He is pictured urinating off the stage at the opening of a creative writing school named in his honour, for example, an action that convinced Orr that the job of looking after Lawrence's reputation involved stifling, wherever possible, the actual Lawrence. The emergence of 'Patrick's' tapes is what concerns Orr most of all—the truth, despite the trust's best efforts, might get out. This is especially the case when the recordings end up in the hands of Geneva Trott, Orr's *bête noire*, a woman who years back wrote an 'unauthorised biography of sorts' in 'a tired life-and-works series that was a graveyard for third-rate lit-crits and (usually) tenth-rate writers'.

So far so good: we have a sadistic novelist who has wrecked the lives of his hangers-on, and we have a blind public, whom the hangers-on spend much of their time trying to mislead. As a story this much is well told, and amid the darkness there is considerable light and humour. There is something much more significant about the book, though—something that is deeply troubling. C.K. Stead never quite got to this in his review in the online magazine *The Spinoff*, even if he hinted at it: 'It is slightly embarrassing to spell all this out,' he wrote after a lengthy summary of the plot. 'There is something so dingy about it all.' What is 'dingy' is the novel's inquiry into the politics and power of art, specifically the way that it asks whether art in its moment of greatest achievement is terrible for us and terrible for others. It is not literature to live by, in other words, but quite the opposite: a pitiless form of writing that will end living as we know it.

The reference in the novel to Cavafy's 'Waiting for the Barbarians' offers some suggestion as to what the author is doing. Lawrence's fourteen-year-old mistress says she is 'like those women in the Cavafy poem', who 'can't wait for the barbarians to come'. In the poem itself, everyone finds themselves disappointed when the hordes fail to arrive: 'Now what's going to happen to us without barbarians?' they ask. 'Those people were a kind of solution.' We await being overrun by the barbarians, the logic runs, we crave the overwhelming presence of Lawrence and the force of his fiction.

Possession, dominance, mastery, and the origins and capacities of powerful art: that is what this novel is about. Even as Lawrence takes control of people for his own purposes, destroying them with his hateful, loving attention, we realise that this is the 'crime', in Lawrence's words, out of which all great art is made. What is the point of what Lawrence calls 'all these fucking lady writers', the 'shit people write about their hip operations—art as therapy, tomorrow will be another day, all that weak shit'? Art, more properly, should be 'poison'. (It is in this spirit that Lawrence declares that his writing school, if he's going to be forced to have one, will be placed in the men's toilets—'Only place for it!') Yet having a supra-ethical, Nietzschean view of literature leaves victims strewn across the novel, banal and fallen as they no doubt are. Orr thinks that without Lawrence he would 'never have walked with gods'. The problem, which is addressed repeatedly, is whether this could ever be an exchange worth the making—the costs of Leda's encounter with the Swan.

One of the tasks of the book, then, is to learn to wrestle with what Orr calls the 'destructive element', the 'order of fiction that is … unforgivable, almost criminal':

> That Jerzy Kosinski novel … where a boy watches a man's eyes being gouged out with a spoon. The scene in which Major Marvy is castrated in *Gravity's Rainbow* … Thomas Bernhard, everything of his that I know in English—*The Lime Works*, with its terrible opening scene, all those people covered in excrement. There's a short story … in which a man eats part of his own prolapsed innards, slowly, and in detail. And then there's always *Naked Lunch*. So many more as well—and in all of them, genius and evil crouched together in the dung, conspiring, the one thing, inseparable. Hell itself.

Here, finally, writing means something other than our petty squabbles, pushing beyond our trivial concerns. Instead, we face 'the dung', 'hell itself'.

This presents a political problem, of course: what is the value of writing that promotes not what we could call 'democratic' affects but ones relating more to power and overcoming? What should we read books for, if not for the kind of society they could help produce, the kind of people they can make us be? The relationship between the most powerful aesthetic experiences and liberation politics is here put under a particular pressure. For Evans, an author who has spent his career watching the rise and fall of various critical movements—Cambridge School in the Colonies, Theory, and Postcolonialism, to name a few—the messy problem of power and politics remains unresolved. If we are to trust his last critical book, *The Long Forgetting*, literature in New Zealand has much to answer for; it is not until his last chapter, 'Resisting', that we get the sense that fiction and poetry are much other than a guilty colonial discourse. He in fact explicitly calls for a literature that is 'less ideologically informed', and more 'questioning, challenging, innovative, even fun to read'. *The Back of His Head* is serenely unconcerned with proving itself to be resistant to anything other than the political stories we tell about literature. Justice, redress and ideology are quite outside its purview, and art is, if anything, on the side of savagery.

These are old squabbles: William Hazlitt, writing of our divided 'aristocratical' and 'republican' faculties, puts poetry within the former camp, explaining that 'the language of poetry naturally falls in with the language of power'—'Carnage is [poetry's] daughter,' he finds. Lionel Trilling in his reading of Henry James' *The Princess Casamassima* cites Hazlitt, writing:

> We are likely not to want to agree with Hazlitt; we prefer to speak of art as if it lived in a white bungalow with a garden, had a wife and two children, and were harmless and quiet and co-operative. But James is of Hazlitt's opinion; his first great revelation of art came as an analogy with the triumphs of the world; art spoke to him of the imperious will, with the music of an army with banners.

Where for Trilling, 'what art suggests of the glorious life' must be tempered by political morality that eschews 'coercive power', *The Back of His Head* asks us what kind of politics could possibly restrain the power of art. Inevitably, this is a challenge to contemporary reading practices: it remains an open question how we can read in a way that does not trivialise or banalise what art can do, and one suspects that Evans has little interest in formulating anything that would come close to an answer. He's too busy watching people's eyes get gouged out with spoons.

Yet such inflated rhetoric can only last so long before it is deflated again, brought back down to earth. We watch as Orr himself spends much of the novel attempting to domesticate Lawrence for a narrative of national self-assertion, a narrative that Lawrence would have utterly rejected. The author was the 'first in our little country to win the greatest prize of all', Orr writes, and 'each of us remembers and remembers and remembers' that time of 'overwhelming excitement'.

The point at which it is all brought down with a crashing thump, though, is when, in the later pages of the novel, the trustees begin to discover that the Master has plagiarised much of his great work. Orr burns the piles of manuscripts and books, all the evidence that the Master may have been nothing but a master thief, in his attempt to leave in abeyance the question of whether the sadism, abuse and torture might have been for nothing after all. And in this last moment Lawrence is truly forgotten, made into something else, as Orr ignores the only lesson his uncle was capable of teaching him: burn the whole lot, published and unpublished, Lawrence would have said. Forget me entirely and maybe then you will finally become yourself.

The last words are given over to the critics who have failed to make sense of Lawrence, words that themselves haunt attempts to begin the process of domestication (of which this review is one of the first acts). Trott's urge to smooth the Lawrence story into one that asks nothing of us shares much with the job of the critic, resounding darkly of the biographical readings that have long been undertaken in Janet Frame's work, both by Evans and others. It is a kind of entrapment—the very entrapment that Evans himself has written of—as he invites his readers, especially those who would be hostile to him, to search for phantasms of ourselves, and to be as banal as we can be.

More than that, though, it is the working out of the problems of writing from within the house of someone else's fiction and being a person made up out of other people's writing. It is a novel that in significant ways is about what it means to be the author of *Gifted*, and what it means to have encountered literature across a lifetime. Evans, after all, was correct when he wrote on *The Spinoff* that *The Back of His Head* 'reads like a parable of reading': the novel is a parable, or perhaps a cautionary tale, of what all that reading has wrought.

Something Rich and Strange

by Kirstine Moffat

The Chimes, by Anna Smaill (Sceptre, 2015), 291pp, $28

To plunge into the world of Anna Smaill's *The Chimes* is to be disoriented and unsettled. This sense of what Darko Suvin terms 'cognitive estrangement' is a core feature of dystopian writing; witness Ray Bradbury's inversion of the firefighter in *Fahrenheit 451*, the douser of flames becoming the igniter of fires, or George Orwell's opening to *Nineteen Eighty Four*: 'It was a bright cold day in April, and the clocks were striking thirteen.' In *The Chimes* music has become a terrifying, omnipresent weapon. The novel is set in an alternate England, where written words and memory are banned. Everything is controlled by an immense Carillon whose majestic Chimes create acoustic vibrations that result in 'memoryloss' for the populace.

In a parody or echo of church ritual, the Chimes ring out morning and night. At Matins 'OneStory' is told, the official version of 'Allbreaking', the 'dischord' that shattered time past and created time present. At evening Vespers the Chimes pour forth music at such an unbearable pitch that listeners are overwhelmed to the point of losing their memories. 'There is no space for any other thought' than the music, which 'is like a fist'. The result is a collective amnesia, a world in which people rely on the ingrained habits of 'bodymemory'. Without the lifeline of a regular routine and familiar places, minds disintegrate and people drift, lost and alone. The terrible Chimes can also result in physical degeneration, triggering shaking and eventually collapse and death.

The Carillon and the Chimes it produces are controlled by the mysterious 'Order'. Based in Oxford they have managed to insulate themselves from the effect of the chimes they use to control others through the rare silvery metal palladium. In a microcosm removed from dystopian reality they live in a seemingly perfect musical utopia, creating ever more intricate harmonies for the great Carillon.

But this utopian microcosm exists at an unbearable cost for others. The past is a foggy mystery, the time before Allbreaking characterised as 'blasphony'. All that is left is today, and each day is the same as the last. This terrible evocation of a continuous 'now' acts as a subtle critique of contemporary Western society, so preoccupied with the desires of the moment that past, present and future blur. Smaill's novel is a reminder of the necessity of history, both the small, poignant histories of individual lives and the weaving together of a collective narrative of origin and belonging. Without this awareness of the past, of before, there can be no future. The wonderful Shakespearean word 'hereafter' resonates through the text, the protagonist Simon daring to dream of a world that is different, a world of possibility.

There are lots of Shakespearean echoes in *The Chimes*, references to *Hamlet* and *Macbeth*, and other fragments, such as 'Patience on a monument' from *Twelfth Night*. These work both as a powerful reminder of the importance of words as a means of spoken and written communication, and as part of the pattern of overlapping time periods that add to the disorientation of the reader. This temporal dislocation is produced by an interweaving of hints and allusions. The vast Carillon and the London landscape completely devoid of technology have a medieval flavour. Yet references to Shakespeare, Buxtehude and Brahms locate the reader in a world of evolving literary and musical taste.

The orphan Simon finds a home with the Five Rover 'pact', a group of outlaws who eke out a living from the tunnels under the Thames by collecting fragments of palladium. These riverscapes and the community of orphans evoke Dickens and are also reminiscent of Joan Aiken's *Midnight is a Place*. Simon finds warmth and comfort in a worn 'burberry' but also wears jeans, placing the reader in a world that is partly familiar but mostly strange. The way forward for Simon emerges through a network of allusions to Norse mythology, in particular the ravens Huginn and Muninn, adding a timeless, mythic dimension.

The parallel with Aiken points to another key aspect of the novel: a focus on young adults as the potential source of salvation. This is not a young-adult novel, but it does share some of the tropes of that genre. The teenage protagonist Simon is (like Katniss Everdeen or Harry Potter) exceptional, for he has inherited the gift of being able to see his memories by holding an 'objectmemory' in which his most precious remembrances are stored. During the course of the novel he discovers that he also has the capacity to see other people's memories by touching their objectmemories. He is encouraged in his role as a memory keeper by the blind musician Lucien, who has escaped from the Order and yearns to bring about change.

Dystopian narratives are frequently shot through with utopian possibility, the traveller becoming gradually aware of the evils of the society they inhabit and, on occasion, actively striving to effect change. In some texts, such as *Nineteen Eighty Four* or Aldous Huxley's *Brave New World*, this utopian yearning is cruelly snuffed out. In others, such as *Fahrenheit 451* or Margaret Atwood's *The Handmaid's Tale*, there is some hope for change. What links *The Chimes* most closely to young adult dystopias like *The Hunger Games* and *Divergent* is its use of the young heroes as forces of optimism and rebellion, capable of dreaming the really big dream of destroying the Carillon. As the novel progresses, the slow pace escalates and the narrative rushes to its climax.

The Chimes is also a love story, tender and understated. The growing sense of the emotional bond and physical intimacy between Simon and Lucien adds to the feeling of hope and also the profound awareness of the fragility of life and the enormous capacity there is for hurt when we let others get close. Simon muses of love: 'What else opens up your veins like that, pulls the sky in, fish hooks the stars into such brightness.'

Smaill is a poet as well as a novelist and The Chimes is written in a mesmerising poetic prose. It's a challenge to give a sense of a world in which sound is everything when constrained by the medium of words on a page. Smaill, herself a violinist, evokes the aural through the use of musical terms to describe speed and movement. Characters 'turn presto' and 'move lento'. The solfege—doh ray me fah soh lah te—has become a sign language through which people communicate. Throughout, the poetic words conjure the power of music to stir and to overwhelm:

> The chords wash over. They clean and centre me. The weight of the tonic goes down my spine and into the ground.

> Follow the melody through its variations, through its opening and flowering. It tells of harmony and beauty. It tells of a beauty wider than any of us.

Dystopia is one of the genres of the moment. What is so remarkable about The Chimes is the way in which familiar themes and tropes are handled with originality and inventiveness. To return to Shakespeare, who is a lingering trace in the narrative, Smaill creates a novel that is beautifully 'rich and strange'.

Bright Glimpses
by Thom Conroy

Trifecta, by Ian Wedde (Victoria University Press, 2015), 175pp, $30

A single narrative told across three linked novellas, Trifecta is the latest offering from Ian Wedde, author of over 20 books of poetry, fiction and, more recently, a non-fiction memoir, The Grass Catcher: A digression about home. Trifecta is narrated by the three later-middle-aged children of the fictional Nazi-refugee architect Martin Klepka. The three sections—each is named after one of the Klepka children, Mick, Veronica and Sandy— intersect and overlap to tell the fractured but single story of the fallout from an eccentric, consequential and seriously damaged childhood.

Each novella of Trifecta is its own experiment in voice, its own dense tangle of interiority filtered through the perspective, by turns insightful and myopic, of a uniquely ravaged character. Told in the well-torqued and finely tuned patois of an ageing streetwise Wellington bachelor, Mick's story comes first in the book. This placing is both necessary and unfortunate. It is necessary for a reason that is spoiler-related (and therefore, for this reviewer, *verboten*), but it is also necessary because it is Mick who functions as the book's unlikely narrative centre. Mick was his father's favourite, and is the only sibling to remain in the family home, the famous *Der rote Würfel* or Red Cube house (the design of which Martin senior pilfered from his Modernist compatriot, Farkas Molnár). The placing of Mick's narrative is unfortunate, however, because it is his voice that most charms, niggles and enchants.

Although both Veronica and Sandy are linguistically endowed and downright snappish gabbers, their argot edges toward affectation beside the sententious incision of Mick. A paragraph in his head is worth a page or two anywhere else in *Trifecta*. Listen to him think as he pops into the TAB to place a trifecta bet, his brain mulling over an encounter with a street preacher and the news item he read about a recuperating racehorse called Maestro:

> Inside, I put five grand on a Final Touch, Xanadu and Burgundy trifecta for the Trentham Telegraph this afternoon. The sound of thousands of tiny burning Bibles. Maestro grazing the sweet grass of his home paddock, out of the running, no chance. It's got nothing to do with belief. Burn it. Cauterise it. Burn the Bibles. That peptide rush of certainty. When in doubt, don't.

All of our time in Mick's company is spicy and brisk. Wedde crafts the voice of Mick—an endorphically grounded creature of the body in contrast to his more emotional sister and cerebral brother—out of such treacly syntax that it's almost unfailingly delicious.

On its own, Mick's voice could carry the narrative, and I, for one, was sad to see him yield the floor to Veronica. Veronica, it should be said, does emerge as a fully realised and intricate character. What's more, of the three narrators, she is the most sympathetic, simply because, as she herself is well aware, she is concerned with the care of others. Nonetheless, after the high-octane monologue of Mick, her voice amounts to a tapering off.

Sandy, the final *Trifecta* narrator, is a solipsistic and self-righteous gasbag. Yes, he is perfectly aware of this fact, and yes, he is capable of old-school character transformation, but even so, seeing the world through his eyes can leave you with an ache in your intellectual seat. Plotwise, Wedde may have had little choice but to conclude with Sandy's perspective, but the shift from Mick to Veronica to Sandy marks a downward trend in terms of sheer reading pleasure.

When Victoria University Press's *These Rough Notes* asked Wedde if he could 'talk about the decision to tell the story from the [point-of-view of the] three siblings', the author's reply drew attention to the 'manageable number of points-of-view and voices' as well as 'the narrative disjunction' between those voices. The three narrators, Wedde explained, allow for 'the development of strongly distinguished characters who, however, can remain in sight of each other in terms of relationship—their triangulation can be both intimate and alienating'.

In many ways, *Trifecta* seems to be about the way perspective alters truth. The same street preacher to whom Mick gifts a pack of cigarettes, for instance,

Sandy walks past with disdain. Similarly, both brothers recall the scene of Sandy encountering Mick and Martin outside the Freyberg Pool in Wellington. In Mick's version, Sandy pretends not to notice them, while, when Sandy recalls it, he's sure that Mick and his father don't see him. The point seems to be that the truth of reality is as knotted and thorny as each of the subjectivities Wedde renders in its own inimitable voice.

A surprisingly beautiful line occurs—and recurs—to Sandy during the final story: 'How do we open up to these bright glimpses of another world than ours?' If each point of view in the book constitutes its own world, then this question emerges as a kind of thematic pivot on which the trilogy of stories turn: the three perspectives offer three equivocal visions of another reality. It is this same concern with opening up to glimpses into the world of another that seems to concern Wedde as he discusses his writerly approach in the interview above. In *Trifecta* such glimpses sometimes go unnoticed, but when characters recognise the encounter with another world, the effect be can be jarring, confusing and, more rarely, illuminating.

A 'trifecta' is a race in which the person betting forecasts the first three finishers in a race in the correct order. The finishers in this book are clear enough, but what remains ambiguous is exactly what it is they're finishing, and what it might mean to win such a race: are the three ageing siblings racing toward death or redemption? Equally important seems to be the question of whose world it is in which the winning takes place. Sandy's question—How do we open up to these bright glimpses of another world than ours?—strikes me as the central refrain of Wedde's book, as each narrative appears to be shaped around the loss or discovery of another world than his or her own.

Trifecta seems grounded in this question of lost connections, of the challenge in sharing reality across estranged perspectives. If the book itself might be said to perform a version of this question as it relates to the reader, then what remains unfocused for me is what answers are available, either to the characters or to us.

The Psychopathic God
by Jack Ross

R.H.I., by Tim Corballis (Victoria University Press, 2015), 208pp, $30

> It reminded me of the idea of a language game that the philosopher Wittgenstein used to talk about, not really meaning that language games were things that happened but that language is like a game, and that we play games with who we are and with our language, not real games but that it's all make believe, even if it's not. (pp. 22–23)

In many ways it's easier to say what Tim Corballis's new book *isn't* than what it is. It certainly doesn't constitute a conventional novel, even by the most liberal definition. Nor, really, do its two discrete sections operate as independent (or even co-dependent) novellas. They're much stranger and more fragmentary than that.

The author claims to detect in his own work 'a history of the twentieth century'—albeit an 'incomplete' one, 'produced by accident'—but working out precisely what he means by that is almost as complex as trying to make sense of the stories themselves (if they really *are* stories—sustained pieces of make-believe—that is).

> Having started I had to carry on. Doing what? … I had to admit that I was here mostly for a warm place to sit.

How true that is of so much research, particularly in those strange repositories of obsolete intellectual endeavour called archives. Corballis has clearly caught the archival bug with a vengeance, but the larger significance of the bits and pieces of information he unearthed in Berlin and London, and (later) back home in New Zealand, seems mostly to have emerged in retrospect.

There's a revealing remark near the beginning of the second novella, 'H':

> Did the sense of a PRESENCE simply grow out of my research? It should be clear that I absolutely do not believe in ghosts, or in any kind of special paranormal sensitivity on my part—these documents are the products of an ordinary person, and at times seem like simply diaries, at others like works of fiction, and at others still like the rough notes of a historian or biographer.

I share Corballis's fascination with the early history of the psychoanalytical movement, and the curious texture of his prose—the almost Janet-and-John-like simplicity of alternating questions and answers—does have the effect of recreating something of the rather uncanny atmosphere surrounding these pioneers in the unmapped regions of the unconscious.

It's hard, then, to believe that he means this disavowal of the reality of the 'floating agents' (as he calls them, though he also refers to them as 'ghosts') to be taken entirely at face value. The idea that a too-vehement negation of any proposition is a clue that its author secretly suspects the opposite is one of the most familiar truisms in the Freudian lexicon, and it's probably also the one that operates best as a rule of thumb in everyday life.

I take with a considerable grain of salt our author's claim to be 'an ordinary person'. I don't think we would bother with these notes if they were purely the product of random gleanings in the archives. A considerable amount of shaping intelligence has been devoted to these twin stories, or assemblages, or collages, or whatever you want to call them.

Part One, 'R', about Joan R (or Joan Riviere) and her various experiences before and after the First World War, is probably the more approachable of the two. The territory it investigates is familiar enough from such works as Pat Barker's *Regeneration*, or (to go back a bit further) D.M. Thomas's *The White Hotel*.

Naming these precedents does have the effect of isolating some of the oddness in Corballis's method, however. The tales these two earlier authors tell are still, recognisably, novels: fictional recreations of the past—the compositions of true believers in the value of make-believe.

It's hard to believe that Corballis is simply failing to carry out a similarly seamless act of retrieval and reconstruction. It's far more probable that these roughnesses and jump-cuts and refusals to round off his narrative strands are due to a loss of faith in what Lallans poet Hugh MacDiarmid once referred to as 'the haill clanjamfrie'.

And, if one accepts this hypothesis, the structure of Corballis's book begins at once to make more sense. Part Two, 'H', about the German architect Hermann Henselmann, takes us straight into the aftermath of another war, amid the ruins of postwar Berlin.

After the proclamation of the death of God by Nietzsche in the 1880s (whether you attribute the act itself to him, to Darwinism, or to Scientific Method itself), the two principal belief systems that have dominated the modern age are undoubtedly Marxism, the idea of history as a shaping force, interpreted by its own priesthood the Communist Party; and Psychoanalysis, the study of the unconscious, the shaping force behind the seemingly irrational and inexplicable acts that dominate human lives.

Joan R's failed analysis with Ernest Jones, Freud's biographer and his first English disciple, dramatises her own conflict with the absolute faith required of adherents to the psychoanalytic cause (studded, like so many dogmatic systems, with great heresies and expulsions from the pure stream of belief: Adler, Jung, Otto Rank …).

One of the most amusing strands in Hermann H's story is his own series of on-again, off-again attempts to flee to West Berlin. He talks his girlfriend, Anita R, into coming with him, then is swayed into staying by her counter-arguments, only to find that she's now decided to go, leading him to decide to accompany her, only to find that she's now been persuaded by his own misgivings to stay, and so on and so forth, the whole accompanied by ironic interpolations by Bertolt Brecht.

Faith, once again, is at the root of it all. As H makes his little compromises, deciding to go along with the purging of a colleague, to accept the (considerable) leg-up it offers him, we observe first hand his attempts to keep alive the flame of the new Utopia that might rise from these ruins: the architectural solution it might offer to the problem of man's inhumanity to man.

There's nothing here (except by implication) about the Stasi, no attempt to dramatise—as in Gunter Grass's *The Plebeians Rehearse the Uprising*—the irony of Brecht's staging a play about proletarian revolt while the workers are literally fighting and dying in the streets outside his theatre. This is not that sort of story.

It's hard, at times, to avoid a snort of contemptuous disbelief as the characters in Corballis's story attribute the continuing disunity of Germany to the West's callous refusal to accept Stalin's grand proposal for reunification. And yet that very scepticism is, I suppose, the point.

There's nothing easier than to write po-faced books of 'warnings from the past' like Martin Amis's *Koba the Dread*. Harder, much harder, is to recreate that atmosphere of the true (albeit, at times, wavering) believer. Corballis's virtue is his refusal to editorialise, to put facts in their 'true perspective', to supply the party line on what we now 'know' to be true.

What he's created is, I suppose, a kind of anti-narrative: not so much a Freudian case-study, in which the details are all eventually supposed to cohere into a larger reading, or even a Marxist analysis of the economic and class relationships of the various 'floating agents' whom we are forced by narrative convention (perhaps F.R. Leavis might provide a third member of his trinity, to set beside Freud and Marx) to regard as fictional 'characters'.

Psychoanalysis took its emphasis from the devastation of the First World War. What was, before, an intellectual movement confined to the examination of the neuroses of certain wealthy members of the middle classes in Mitteleuropa, spread to England and America largely as an antidote to the shell-shock and despair of the lost generation.

The inability of psychoanalysts to diagnose Europe's ills sufficiently to prevent yet another war did rather put paid to that particular system of faith: *What huge imago made/ A psychopathic god*, as W.H. Auden presciently asks in his poem 'September 1, 1939'.

Marxism is treated in a rather more allusive way in Corballlis's second section: partly, I suppose, due to its far greater longevity ('A spectre is haunting Europe—the spectre of Communism' is a statement that dates back to the *Communist Manifesto* of 1848). Also, perhaps, because it needs less fleshing out—and refutation—for contemporary readers.

Corballis's book, then, part fiction, part history, part archival research, part imaginative projection is (at any rate in this reading) an attempt to analyse *all* these losses of faith: faith in ideologies that probably never deserved it in the first place, but which nevertheless started off as attempts to taxonomise and interpret the realities around us, only to end up as codified sets of dogmas, valuable only as control mechanisms for the masses.

It's hard, too, to argue too vigorously with Corballis's loss of faith in fiction itself. What is left, after all, of all those Leavisite claims about the English Department as the 'natural centre of a university'—of the function of literature to promote alert, enquiring minds within healthy, organic communities? Little enough, I fear.

'By their fruits ye shall know them,' says the Gospel of Matthew, of Jesus's followers. I'm afraid that Gibbon's *Rise and Fall of the Roman Empire* put paid to any naïve notions we might have that the warring communities of the early church showed any greater charity to one another than was meted out to them by emperors such as Commodus or Domitian.

'Great Marxist Humanitarians'—that was one of Kingsley Amis's suggestions for the world's shortest book. I guess one could add 'The Tolerance of Dissent within the Psychoanalytic Movement' and 'Lives of the Saintly Literature Professors' as alternative candidates.

But even if these systems of faith now seem less compelling than absurd, what is one left with once they're gone? The pen may still be moving across the paper in Corballis's increasingly bleak and Beckettian universe, but one can't help but wonder for how long?

And yet, is his dilemma so very different from that of Matthew Arnold in 'Dover Beach'?:

> The Sea of Faith
> Was once, too, at the full, and round earth's shore
> Lay like the folds of a bright girdle furled.
> But now I only hear
> Its melancholy, long, withdrawing roar,
> Retreating, to the breath
> Of the night-wind, down the vast edges drear
> And naked shingles of the world.

Corballis has reminded us just how dark and inhospitable those 'naked shingles of the world' can be, but also how fascinating and various. There's always been something a bit unconvincing about the resolution of Arnold's poem: 'Ah, love, let us be true/ To one another!' The despair in his poem speaks louder.

Corballis, a hundred years on, may have more ruins to survey, but his solution—to delve and to taxonomise—remains, I have to admit, the best we have.

In Their Ruin
by David Herkt

The Fixer, by John Daniell (Upstart Press, 2015), 288pp, $34.99

'I see the boys of summer in their ruin/ lay the gold tithings barren ...' wrote Dylan Thomas in his first book of poems in 1934. It seems an apt pair of fateful lines to summarise the lives and careers of so many of New Zealand's prominent sporting figures: the early promise, the seasonal flourish, the celebrity and the inevitability of decline. It is also a set of circumstances that have bred knowing human attitudes, if not media headlines, as once-feted sporting luminaries plunge into scandal, bankruptcy, divorce and serial marriage, or worse. In its essence, for a country that so prides itself on its on-field prowess, this narrative progress has become the quintessential contemporary New Zealand story.

John Daniell was born and educated in New Zealand, but is also a graduate in English from Oxford University. He is the author of *Inside French Rugby: Confessions of a Kiwi mercenary*, which won the Best Rugby Book section of the British Sports Book Awards in 2010. It was an autobiographical account of Daniell's decade playing rugby for the Racing, Perpignon and Montpellier clubs in southern France between 1996 and 2006. It was a true rugby fan's book, providing a completely fresh insight into the mercenary teams, the hand-picked 'combat-troops' who have populated the European rugby world since the sport went professional in the mid-1990s.

Inside French Rugby was not the clumsily ghost-written, game-by-game biographical glimpse that is familiar to readers of books devoted to the sport. Daniell's view was one of gladiatorial games, with players from various countries, barely speaking a common tongue, and schedules almost inhumane in their demands from muscle and bone. He depicted trained bodies at the mercy of the decisions of coaches, management and distant financiers with their own business or political agendas. For Daniell, rugby was no longer a game about honour, but was a spectacle about endurance, money and prestige.

Inside French Rugby also presented a gruelling view of Daniell's last season as a representative European player, and this story arc has been neatly transferred to his recent novel, *The Fixer*. This is fiction, as is frequently said, 'right out of today's headlines', a fact that provides much of its interest.

The protagonist of *The Fixer*, Mark Stevens, is a New Zealand rugby player, a former All Black who has been playing in France but is facing the end of his playing career. He is 32, and the weight of accumulated small cartilage injuries is beginning to tell. He's only making it through every game with the barely legal administration of a pre-match painkiller.

There is also his future to consider. He's divorced. His sister in New Zealand is dependent on the money he sends. Investments have gone belly up. He's also met a beautiful Argentinian journalist, Rachel Da Silva, but along with her obvious attractions for Stevens, including a dragon tattoo extending upwards from her buttock's cleft, she also has quite another offer to make in a world that is happy to bet big money on small features of matches. It begins slowly with a gifted Rolex in exchange for a casual game assessment of point-spread, but escalates swiftly into something more corrupt and threatening.

Any follower of the scandals and legal trials that have enveloped professional cricket, especially in India over recent years, will immediately see the relationship of Stevens' predicament to those events. The problematic figure of cricketer Chris Cairns looms behind the narrative. Game-fixing provides the central moral quandary of this novel, and Daniell inches into it with aplomb, setting up his situations and neatly locking the reader into an inevitable and believable ethical conflict.

He is not a natural fiction writer, however. A reader who has read both *Inside French Rugby* and *The Fixer* will appreciate that the best insights of *The Fixer* have their basis in Daniell's own career in France, and indeed, in all probability, the act of writing *Inside French Rugby* itself. In many ways—in terms of background and detail—they are the same book. One informs the other, although *The Fixer* plunges into a hypothetical world of 'what if' with an added dose of steroids.

Both books, despite their ostensible differences, are playing against time. *Inside French Rugby*, with its basis in reality, does it better. It is a vastly more human book. It makes palpable the problems of age, younger players and injury. *The Fixer*, with its fictional freedom, might dramatise but it cannot equal the weight of veracity.

There is also the problem of structure in *The Fixer*. Daniell runs two plot-streams: one features Stevens in his last year of professional rugby, the other focuses on his grandfather, a soldier fighting the Germans during the First World War on French battlefields, conveyed through journals and an old tape-recorded interview. This emphasises, perhaps too neatly, an analogy between rugby players and soldiers as pawns in a game. It is also somewhat of a diversionary tactic that serves neither narrative well.

Daniell has done his research, from his own grandfather's account of the Somme to books on Ettie Rout, the prophylactic pioneer whose work giving condoms to soldiers saved many from venereal disease. However, the whole First World War strand of the *The Fixer* remains separate and structurally marooned, as both a device of comparison and a plot-line. It might thicken the novel but it does not illuminate. It is somehow unnecessary.

Stevens' voice is authentic, or feels so. His other characters, from Da Silva, the

Brazilian journalist, to his bawdy teammates, barely rise above stock casting. Da Silva remains the glamorous femme fatale with her pert, always available body. Stevens' fellow players blur. The villain of the piece is an enigma to the last pages and none of the final developments really assists any humanising of his role.

It cannot be doubted that Daniell can write both entertainingly and informatively. His dialogue is frequently engaging, nicely colloquial, and rattled off at a pace. He makes a good case that every rugby player should have a degree in English: this education has vastly assisted him in his game descriptions. He also has a sense of literary pace. His faint echoes of William Carlos Williams and other Modernist poets are wry and serve him well, strengthening his text in interesting ways; *The Fixer* actually begins with the line 'So much depends upon an oval white ball.'

Unfortunately none of these skills can disguise the fact that *The Fixer* smells too much of construction. It is a book that begs to be let free from its form, its intended popular readership and imagined bestseller lists. Daniell is much better than this. He is uniquely placed to be able to write a great New Zealand rugby novel, so it is particularly regrettable to this reader that *The Fixer* isn't it.

Money
by Elizabeth Heritage

Credit in the Straight World, by Brannavan Gnanalingam (Lawrence & Gibson, 2015), 244pp, $23

Credit in the Straight World is a satirical account of the global financial crisis (GFC) narrated through the rise and fall of a fictional finance company, Manchester Gold (loosely based on South Canterbury Finance). Told in the first person, the novel is narrated by George Tolland, who is largely concerned with telling the life story of his financier brother Frank (loosely based on Allan Hubbard), from the time of the Great Depression up until the GFC. *Credit* is set in Manchester, a fictitious but very recognisable small Kiwi town in Canterbury.

On one level, Gnanalingam succeeds very well. In an interview broadcast on RNZ National, he explains that he worked as a lawyer throughout the GFC, specifically handling the collapses of failing finance companies. The legal and financial details—the way Frank sets up and manages (or mismanages) Manchester Gold—feel realistic, and well drawn. Gnanalingam illustrates clearly the human frailty and irrationality inherent in our financial systems, and particularly the roles played by trust and blind faith. I was struck by the scene in which the people of Manchester respond to the impending prosecution of Frank (for essentially defrauding the entire town) by holding a parade in his honour. George muses on the nature of money:

> It seemed to me money was nothing more than a language, something that simply governs our social interactions like words and phrases, that like words it doesn't coalesce in a rational way, it could never materialise yet own a house, or it can be carried along in a wheelbarrow to buy a loaf of bread, and the moment we give it more power than that, the moment we give it a physicality that could be hoarded, or indeed at a basic level belong to somebody, we elevate it beyond its intended station.

Where I feel *Credit* does not succeed is in the reading experience: the narrator's unwavering flat affect and deadpan tone is eventually tiresome. George's sly, caustic delivery starts out as amusing, and the potted history of 'Manchester' in the prologue is entertaining. It reminded me initially of satirist Steve Braunias's *Civilisation*, a collection of essays in which he examines—often to very unflattering effect—small New Zealand towns and their inhabitants. But I gradually came to see that, whereas Braunias's portraits, though sometimes dark and distressing, are always the result of unflinching observation of specific, real people, Gnanalingam's satire is drawn much more broadly: an urban intellectual taking pot-shots at stereotypical rural small-timers.

The people of Manchester are strongly anti-union. George relates how, during the dock strikes, they sent care packages to the company owners. They are sexist: Frank's wife Pauline avoids wearing trousers for fear of appearing not respectable. And so on: Manchesterians love rugby (but only when played by men), always elect the conservative candidate unopposed, and are embarrassingly behind the times. They are white and unwelcoming of people who are not; they are violently jingoistic and display a nationalistic patriotism of the most toxic kind.

One of the big problems for me in reading *Credit*, then, was the dearth of likeable or sympathetic characters. Partly this is because Gnanalingam was setting out to illustrate how a combination of greed, stupidity and wilful ignorance caused the GFC, so this was never going to be a happy story. Mostly, though, I just found spending time in George's head to be unpleasant and dull. Frank is a crook and a plodding bore whose fate I found it very hard to care about, and George is so entirely passive that he seems to hardly be physically present in Manchester at all. Gnanalingam says he purposely made George deaf and mute to illustrate the way people invest their money blindly, but the result is that the narrator is so dissociated from the world around him that I felt unengaged too.

I kept waiting for *Credit* to fulfil its satirical potential by delivering fresh insights—into New Zealandness, into behavioural economics, into how GFCs in future can be avoided—I'm not even sure what. I was thrilled when, on page 122, I found one on, of all things, New Zealand art, when George takes a very rare trip outside Manchester to Wellington:

> I wanted to see the national museum, particularly some of the art, the Rita Angus, which upon seeing it, created this strange sense of nostalgia of having lived in it but having missed out on it …

I was pleased to have that insight, since that's the way I feel about a particular kind of New Zealand art as well, but I've never quite been able to put it into words. And if there had been more of that, more times when George puts his head above the parapet and takes a break from his relentless, monotonous snark, I could have forgiven *Credit* a lot more of its flaws.

But even in the example above, that's only the first part of a very long sentence. Apart from the dialogue, which Gnanalingam writes very well, the prose is tiresomely verbose. As his sentences got longer and longer—sometimes half a page or more—I became less and less willing to put in the effort to make sense of them. When, after 244 pages, the book finally finished, I mostly felt relieved, and slightly irked. The dramatic ending, presumably intended as the emotional climax of the book, left me entirely unmoved.

I've been thinking a lot about why I disliked this book so much and the conclusion I've come to is this: I can't shake the feeling that the message of *Credit* is that the people of Manchester have only themselves to blame for having lost all their money because they were so easily taken in—that Frank succeeded because he was surrounded by rustic stupidity. And, since *Credit* is intended as a satire of the GFC, this leads me to the uneasy conclusion that, rather than holding the banks, governments and finance companies responsible for the GFC, *Credit* is saying that we (the ordinary investors) are, ourselves, all to blame.

That is why I think *Credit* is ultimately unsuccessful. Good satire takes aim at the powerful and uses dark humour to tell difficult or unpleasant truths. This work is neither funny nor engaging enough to sustain the long form of a book, and its targets are embarrassingly small fry. Rather than being a satire of the GFC, *Credit* contents itself with mocking a rural community for trusting their local finance company and getting ripped off. Avoid.

They Say You Want a Revolution
by Max Oettli

John Fields Signature Series 1975: Forty images curated by David Langham and exhibited at the Gus Fisher Gallery, Auckland, as part of the Auckland Festival of Photography, 2015

In a world of flare pants, flowing robes, microskirts for the ladies and freak flag hair for the guys, John Fields was a straight man. Slacks, polished shoes, button-down shirts and short-back-and-sides haircut, with an intent expression on his face. A good listener, careful with words.

He was from Gloucester, Massachusetts. He'd learned photography in the US Navy, then at the Massachusetts Institute of Technology, before working as a photographer at Massachusetts General Hospital. He became the photographer at Auckland's Medical School in 1966, following an invitation from an American colleague, and lived in New Zealand for ten years before a dispute with the Department of Inland Revenue about the professional status of art photography led him to leave for Australia, where he lived until his death in 2013.

He was a quiet presence in my barman days in the Kiwi pub, never drunk, and usually at a table of photographers and artists of all kinds, including Gary Baigent, Jim Keogh, Don Gifford and others—cooler, older guys than me. Gary had produced an amazing book of Auckland photographs influenced by Robert Frank, grainy rough pictures in a beautifully designed but rather trashily offset printed volume, *The Unseen City* (1967), published by Blackwood & Janet Paul. I did a rather waspish review of it for *Craccum* the same year, from the height of my twenty years, uneasily conscious of its raw visual power, but growling at Gary Baigent poaching on territory I considered mine, the streets and hidden corners of Auckland, which I was also stalking.

Another photographer who occasionally joined them was Simon Buis. He put up a show in the Wynard Tavern, using a similar approach to Gary's but with a David Bailey swinging London look, betrayed by a sprinkling of leggy ladies against grimy brick walls. This inspired me to put up 70 prints there in early 1970—no leggy ladies, but a few bare grimy brick walls betrayed my existential angst …

I knew by then that Fields was a photographer, and a fine one. He'd been interested in the photography lecturer's job at Elam that eventually went to John B. Turner, and had put up an informal show there which I remember had us pretty impressed with its purity and finesse of vision and a print quality you could fall into.

It was after seeing my Wynard Tavern show, *Visible Evidence*, that John Fields invited me to contribute to the anthology *A Visual Dialect*, a little booklet featuring the work of ten photographers, a kind of exhibition catalogue sans exhibition. There was then nowhere worthwhile to exhibit photos, outside of places like the Wynyard Tavern where, as Tom Hutchins wrote in his *Auckland Star* review of my stuff, one had to 'peer over the heads of coffee drinkers to see' work.

In the *Visual Dialect* booklet John led the charge with a militant introduction:

> Photography is a visual dialect of our times, a method of dialogue between photographers and the society in which they live. Those inherent and unique qualities of photography, as seen in photographs, are no longer a mystery but an affirmation of man's innate ability to restructure pure technology for the expansion of his own creative expression.
>
> For those whose cynicism of the contemporary expressive methods still remains a thing of classic comparatives, the question is invariably asked whether photography is an art; a question in itself quite irrational and overlooking the essence of the issue. It is the individual aesthetic concern and authentic expression that matter, the vehicle of the expression is irrelevant. Photography, as practised by individuals whose sole concern is the principle of photography, deserves more than a casual glance and consideration, it demands a new quality of perception, only then can an appreciation of photography become more than a fortuitous accident of understanding.

Even today, the question 'Is photography an art?' is often raised; a question in itself quite irrational and overlooking the essence of the issue. It is the individual aesthetic concern and authentic expression that matter, the vehicle of the expression is irrelevant. Photography, as practised by individuals determined to express the aesthetic principles of photography, deserves more than a casual glance; it demands appreciative perception.

The polemical nature of Field's above-quoted statement is in the American grain, which brings us back to the expression 'Straight Photography'—the tradition of photographic practitioners such as Alfred Stieglitz, Edward Weston, Paul Strand and Walker Evans—the name for an approach that followed an American 'puritan' ethic based on a profound respect for everyday details and their faithful rendering.

Until the advent of *Photo-Forum* in 1974, writing on New Zealand photography was mostly dismal, with some honourable exceptions such as Frank Hofmann and William Main. I remember gagging on rising bile when I read the blurb to Gary Baigent's book: 'Baigent uses his camera as an artist uses his brush ...'

We can place John in the same basket as Marti Friedlander, Ans Westra, Simon Buis, Robin Morrison, Frank Hofmann and others (I include myself here), who essentially photographed responsively because they were immigrants: outsiders looking in, able to bring a fresh vision to the country of adoption. So it's interesting that the Gus Fisher show and limited edition book offer portraits by

Fields scrutinising the interiors of friends' and colleagues' homes in Auckland.

It was shot with immensely rewarding —in terms of its visual detail—century-old technology over a period of less than a year in 1975. Fields used a large format view camera, 5 x 7 inch, then an 8 x 10 he had acquired through his medical school job, which he mastered with panache and grace, working in carefully graduated black and white. This was a decade before Laurence Aberhart hit the ground hard, lumbering with a similar cumbersome beast.

Fields' series is extraordinary and almost embarrassingly telling of the people involved, who however are never shown, instead presented through their possessions: a kind of forensic record of the then-and-there. Some are the houses of artists, such as Peter and Claudia Pond Eyley, and Pat and Gil Hanly; others exemplify that exciting cultural primordial brew of revolutionary fervour that made Auckland such an exciting environment at that time.

The book presents one-to-one reproductions (unfortunately a little grey, not quite doing justice to JJ's rich tonal palette), in which the last detail is visible, mostly showing interior close-ups, concentrating on that household altar, the mantelpiece, along with details of kitchens, washhouses, beds. For me, the ghosts of these interior photos are mostly personally known and remembered, a kind of cocktail of names; others I feel I may have known four decades ago. There are no strangers here.

Yet I do not entirely feel comfortable with my *unheimlich* intrusions. I feel distinctly uneasy at looking at the bed Don Gifford shared with that beautiful blonde, say, and not just because he has a Lee Enfield rifle next to it. So let's visit the Eyleys: Peter (who used to fix my VW Beetle) and Claudia and their daughter Brigid in their comfortable old Mount Eden house.

Start with the kitchen mantelpiece: its texture, the richness of content in that square metre. There are so many details in the photograph: books, their titles visible evidence of university studies, bringing back memories of English II with Kendrick Smithyman and Karl Stead; American poetry, William Carlos Williams, whose fresh and untrammelled view of reality is very close to photography. History II, with Michael Bassett and Russell Stone on totalitarian regimes, Hitler, Mussolini, Stalin. On walls a nice scattering of pictures, including a Latin American lithograph, its glaring colours tamed by John's carefully managed panchromatic emulsion.

The photograph that looks down the hallway towards the Eyleys' master bedroom is unusual in representing a sense of volume, making depth of vision important, and it also, in its beautiful rendering of light, communicates reluctance by the photographer to intrude further. It's a photographic tour-de-force, with a very wide range of light values, carefully expanded by a system of controlled exposure and individual development of large-format negatives known as the 'Zone System', a technique elaborated on by Ansel Adams and made into an almost mystical and somewhat precious credo by *Aperture* editor and photographer Minor White. John B. Turner made earnest efforts to teach it at Elam; I was too busy with my own street work to get into this little sect.

I look at a different order of visual logic at the Hanlys, where I was used to the chattering of party folks from Elam and the School of Architecture, and feel like an intruder now into a grey silence, into the respect the photograph pays.

I am moved by images of a visit to Dick Scott's place, showing the business of a scholarly militant with a full life, wine, the revolution, a few other components woven into a rich tapestry. Dick Scott it was who gave us a first look at the horror story of Parihaka; his writing asked difficult questions at a critical time. One of his wall decorations is the condemned Fenian Robert Emmet's speech from the dock: *Let no man write my epitaph*. We are overwhelmed by names tacked to the wall at Dick's place, names that are interwoven with the cultural and artistic history of Auckland at the time—Gretchen Albrecht, Emmy Lott, Glenn Busch, Bronwyn Cornish, Bill Rowling, and others on posters and flyers.

One of the things that strikes me, though, is the total absence of music devices, give or take a couple of crappy transistor radios. There were big sound systems—turntables and speakers—in most of these houses, pouring out the Stones, The Who, Pink Floyd, Mahler, Bach through Pioneer or Wharfedale boxes, and there would have been rows of 12-inch LPs neatly stacked in shelves, or possibly strewn on the carpet. Was John, or his photography, tone deaf? What are noticeable are hundreds of books—we were a bookish lot. I count 197 Penguins alone in the 40-odd photographs, to mention only one great publishing house.

So Field's images amount to one of the period's richer collections, showing the contact between photography and the past, bringing it memoriously to life as all the great novelists also do—and in the same way as that which we experience every time we open a family album.

Resurgence Poetry Prize 2016

The World's First Major ECOPOETRY AWARD

NOW IN ITS 2ND YEAR

The Resurgence Poetry Prize is the world's first major 'ecopoetry' award. With a **first prize of £5,000** for the best single poem embracing ecological themes, the award ranks amongst the highest of any English language single poem competition. Second prize is £2,000 and third prize £1,000.

Now in its second year, it was founded in the spring of 2014 by the former UK Poet Laureate Sir Andrew Motion, actress and green campaigner Joanna Lumley, and entrepreneur and environmentalist Peter Phelps. The Resurgence Poetry Prize reflects the founders' shared passion for and commitment to poems that investigate and challenge the interrelationship between nature and human culture.

www.resurgenceprize.org

2nd PRIZE £2000 • 3rd PRIZE £1000
£5000
1st PRIZE
Deadline: 1st October 2016

Opens: 1st June 2016
Closes: 1st October 2016

Fees: First poem: £8
Each additional poem: £3
Please visit
www.resurgenceprize.org
for rules and upcoming details on how to enter online or by post. 2016 Judges will be announced on the website

NEW BOOKS FROM
OTAGO

IN A SLANT LIGHT
A poet's memoir
CILLA MCQUEEN

This account of the life of an extraordinary verbal artist is immensely warm and welcoming. The lightness of Cilla's touch coupled with the grit of her endurance through challenging personal circumstances makes the reader feel privileged to be invited in to the quiet wisdom worn here with both integrity and modesty.

ISBN 978-1-877578-71-7, hardback with ribbon, $50

AS THE VERB TENSES
LYNLEY EDMEADES

'What a fine reminder this collection is, of how language is what memory is played on, and gives the moment its flair, its resonance, its abiding form. I admire As the Verb Tenses for how the past and the present so vividly ring in lines of such clarity and precision and deft witty assessing.'
—Vincent O'Sullivan

ISBN 978-1-927322-25-3, $25

KA NGARO TE REO
Māori language under siege in the 19th century
PAUL MOON

Paul Moon charts the near demise of te reo through the 19th century. Calling on a vast range of published and archival material, Moon probes deeply into the forces of colonisation that pushed te reo perilously close to extinction.

ISBN 978-1-927322-41-3, paperback, $39.95

WOMEN OF THE CATLINS
Life in the deep south
INTERVIEWS: DIANA NOONAN; PHOTOGRAPHS: CRIS ANTONA

'This book is about the way New Zealand used to be, and also about the way New Zealand could yet be. It's about indomitable spirit, true grit, all that stuff. Plus, it's a beautiful thing! Enjoy. Envy. Be inspired.' —Kim Hill

ISBN 978-1-877578-97-7, paperback, $49.95

Otago University Press
From good booksellers or www.otago.ac.nz/press/

THE 2016 UNIVERSITY OF CANBERRA VICE-CHANCELLOR'S INTERNATIONAL
POETRY PRIZE

FIRST PRIZE $15,000
ENTER BY 30 JUNE 2016

The head judge for 2016 will be Simon Armitage.
For more details please visit the prize website:
canberra.edu.au/vcpoetryprize

Recognising creative excellence

UNIVERSITY OF CANBERRA

Tuesday – Friday 11am – 5pm, Saturday 11am – 3pm >>

Blue Oyster art project space.

16 Dowling Street, Dunedin, New Zealand >>

PO Box 5903, Dunedin 9058, New Zealand >>

www.blueoyster.org.nz >>

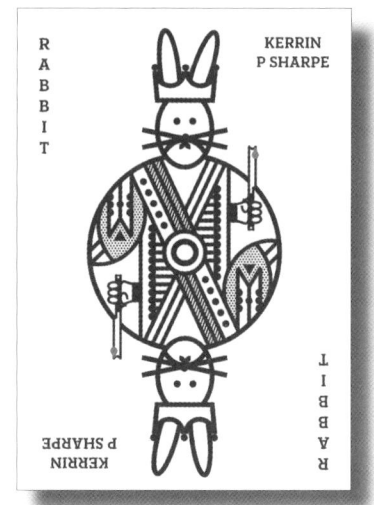

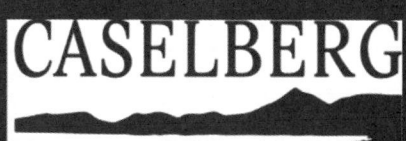

Caselberg Trust International Poetry Prize 2016

First Prize $500
Second Prize $250
5 Highly Commended
(no monetry prize)

Judge: Vincent O'Sullivan

Entry fee
$20 for up to four poems

The first and second placed poems will be published in *Landfall 232* *(Nov. 2016)*

For conditions and entry form, go to
www.caselbergtrust.org

ANNOUNCING THE

BRAND NEW ANNUAL CHARLES BRASCH YOUNG WRITERS' ESSAY COMPETITION

An essay competition for younger writers (aged 16–21).

Essays should be up to 1500 words long and can be on any topic.

Prize: $500 plus a one-year subscription to *Landfall*.

The winning essay will be published in *Landfall*.

Entry details for the 2017 award will be announced in *Landfall 232* (Nov. 2016)

LANDFALL

CONTRIBUTORS

John Adams lives in Auckland. A district court and family court judge since 1995, he has been writing poetry and short stories since 2007. His collection, *Briefcase*, published by AUP, won the 2012 NZSA Jessie Mackay Award for Best First Book of Poetry.

Ruth Arnison lives in Dunedin. Her poems have appeared in various journals, ezines and anthologies in NZ, Australia, the UK and US. She is the editor of *Poems in the Waiting Room* (NZ) and the founder of Lilliput Libraries: lilliputlibraries.wordpress.com

Shelley Arlidge lives in Russell and, until recently, worked there as a museum curator. She's taking a gap year in 2016 to write poems and go tall-ship sailing.

Nick Ascroft lives in Wellington. His third poetry collection, *Back with the Human Condition*, is to be released in late 2016, through VUP.

Liz Breslin lives and writes in Hawea Flat, near Wanaka. Her regular column, 'Thinking Allowed', can be found fortnightly in the *Otago Daily Times*.

Victoria Broome is a Christchurch writer and has been published in various anthologies and journals in NZ. She received the Louis Johnson bursary from Creative NZ in 2005 and was highly commended in the Kathleen Grattan Award in 2010 and 2015. She is a past poetry editor of *Takahē* and works in mental health in primary care in Christchurch.

Janet Charman lives in Auckland and has published seven collections of poetry. Her most recent, *At the White Coast* (AUP, 2012) is a memoir of her year working in London during the Thatcher era.

Stephen Coates is a short story writer who grew up in Christchurch. He currently lives in Japan.

Thom Conroy is a senior lecturer in creative writing at Massey University and a fiction writer whose historical novel, *The Naturalist*, was published in 2014. In 2016 he will publish his second novel, *The Salted Air*.

Jodie Dalgleish is a curator and writer currently based in Luxembourg. After more than a decade in NZ's public galleries, she is focused on cross-genre forms of writing and creative practice.

Andrew Dean is a Rhodes Scholar, currently studying for a doctorate in English literature at the University of Oxford. He is the author of the *Ruth, Roger and Me: Debts and legacies*, published by Bridget Williams Books in 2015.

Bill Direen is a poet, playwright, novelist and singer-songwriter. Educated in Christchurch and currently based in Dunedin, he has spent extensive periods of time in Berlin and France. His books include *Devonport, A Diary* (Holloway Press, 2011) and the novel *Utopia Rag* (Tank Press, 2014).

Doc Drumheller was born in Charleston, South Carolina, and has lived in New Zealand for more than half his life. He has published ten collections of poetry and his poems have been translated into more than twenty languages. He lives in Oxford, where he edits the literary journal *Catalyst* and teaches creative writing at the School for Young Writers.

Johanna Emeney is an Auckland poet and university/senior-school teacher, and recently gained her doctorate from Massey University for her thesis about New Zealand poetry on a medical theme. She works with Ros Ali facilitating the Michael King Young Writers' Programme.

Helen Vivienne Fletcher lives in Wellington. Her poems have appeared in online and print publications. She has recently turned her hand to writing for the stage, and was named Outstanding New Playwright at the Wellington Theatre Awards for her play *How to Catch a Grim Reaper*.

Rata Gordon lives on Waiheke Island and coordinates a creative youth development programme. Her poems have found homes in a number of New Zealand literary journals. She enjoys dancing and tending to her peas.

Siobhan Harvey is the author of *Cloudboy* (Otago University Press, 2014) and co-editor of *Essential New Zealand Poems* (Penguin Random House NZ, 2014). She is a lecturer at the Centre for Creative Writing, Auckland University of Technology. She was shortlisted for the 2015 Janet Frame Memorial Award, won the 2013 Kathleen Grattan Award for Poetry, and was runner-up in the 2015 and 2014 New Zealand Poetry Society International Poetry Competitions.

Elizabeth Heritage is a book reviewer, arts journalist and freelance publishing professional. She is based in Wellington and online at www.elizabethheritage.co.nz

David Herkt is a former TV director and researcher. His TV work has been awarded two Qantas/New Zealand Film and Television Awards. He has published a book of poetry and a number of short stories and autobiographical pieces.

Sam Keenan lives in Wellington. She was the winner of the 2014 Story! Inc. prize for poetry. In 2015 she received an MA in creative writing with distinction from the International Institute of Modern Letters.

Erik Kennedy is originally from New Jersey and now lives in Christchurch. His poems have appeared in *Catalyst*, *Landfall* and *Sport* in New Zealand. He is the poetry editor for *Queen Mob's Teahouse* and is on the board of *Takahē*.

Koenraad Kuiper formerly lectured at the University of Canterbury. His poems have appeared in *Islands*, *Landfall*, *Poetry New Zealand*, *Sport* and *Takahē*. He has published four books of poetry at ten-year intervals: *Signs of Life*, *Mikrokosmos*, *Timepieces* and *Bounty*.

Will Leadbeater is an Auckland-based poet. The author of a number of collections, he is also a former poetry reviewer for the *New Zealand Herald*.

Wes Lee lives in Paekakariki. Her poems have won prizes in the London Magazine's Poetry Competition, the Troubadour Poetry Prize, the New Zealand Society of Authors Poetry Competition and the Printable Reality Poetry Competition, and have been published in magazines including *Cordite*, *Poetry London*, *Magma*, *Meniscus*, *The London Magazine*, *Verandah* and *Westerly*.

Saskia Leek is an artist who lives in Dunedin. She is a former Walter Prize finalist and has exhibited her work widely.

Allison Li studied health psychology at Auckland University and currently works in mental health. She was born in China but considers Auckland her home. Her short fictions have been published in *Potroast*.

Caoimhe McKeogh is based in Wellington where she works as a disability support worker and is a student of English literature at Victoria University.

Robert McLean is a poet and a writer, and a graduate of the University of Canterbury. He lives in Wellington.

Heather McQuillan writes children's stories, flash fiction and poetry. She is a tutor with the School for Young Writers in Christchurch. Her full bio is at http://authors.org.nz/author/heathermcquillan/

Owen Marshall was a 2015 Creative New Zealand–Randell Cottage Writer in Residence. His most recent work of fiction is *Love as a Stranger*, published by Vintage in 2016. He lives in Timaru.

Anthony Millen is the head of English and literacy at Taumarunui High School and has published three novels in the past three years: *Redeeming Brother Murrihy*, *Te Kauhanga* and *The Chain*.

Kirstine Moffat is a senior lecturer in the English programme of the University of Waikato, and the author of *Piano Forte – Stories and Soundscapes from Colonial New Zealand* (Otago University Press, 2012).

Martha Morseth is a Dunedin writer whose poems have been published in the *NZ Listener* and in literary journals. Her second collection of poetry, *Hippopotamus in the Room*, was published in 2012 by Steele Roberts.

Piet Nieuwland is a poet, writer and visual artist who also works on conservation strategies for Te Papa Atawhai. He lives near Whangarei.

Mary Macpherson is a Wellington poet and photographer. Her work has appeared in New Zealand and Australian print and online journals.

Max Oettli is a photographer and researcher based in Geneva. He previously taught photography at the Otago Polytechnic School of Art.

Judy O'Kane works as a solicitor in Dublin. She has published poetry in *The World of Fine Wine*, and in 2015 won the Listowel Writers' Week Original Poem award.

Claire Orchard lives in Wellington. Her poems have appeared in *Landfall*, *Sport*, *JAAM*, *4th Floor*, *Sweet Mammalian*, *Turbine* and *Best New Zealand Poems 2014*. Her first book of poetry, *Cold Water Cure*, was published by VUP in 2016.

Bob Orr has published seven books of poetry, most recently *Odysseus in Woolloomooloo* (Steele Roberts), and his work appears in numerous anthologies. Born in the Waikato, he works as a boatman on the Waitemata Harbour and the Hauraki Gulf. He was awarded the 2016 Lauris Edmond Memorial Award for Poetry.

I.K. Paterson-Harkness grew up in Dunedin and now lives in Auckland. She recently published a novella through Paper Road Press, and has had poems and stories in *JAAM*, *Every Day Fiction*, *Writing Tomorrow*, *Splickety Prime* and *The Kiwi Diary*, to name a few. Twice shortlisted for a Sir Julius Vogel award, she gained a Masters in creative writing from Auckland University in 2012.

Peter Peryer is a photographer based in Taranaki. His works are widely collected and are held in major New Zealand and international institutions, including the Bibliothèque Nationale in Paris and the Australian National Gallery in Canberra.

Vivienne Plumb is of New Zealand and Australian heritage. She writes poetry, fiction and drama and is based in Wellington. She has been the recipient of various NZ awards. A collaboration of her past writing and the work of artist Glenn Otto will be published by split/ fountain publishing, Auckland, in 2016.

Joanna Preston is a Tasmanaut poet and freelance creative writing tutor who lives in semi-rural Canterbury with a flock of chooks and an overgrown garden. She is the poetry editor of *Takahē*.

Jessie Puru is a writer and mother who lives in South Auckland. She is currently a third-year creative writing student at Manukau Institute of Technology.

Vaughan Rapatahana is currently based in the Waikato where he works as an educator. In 2016 he will have books published in the UK, Philippines, Hong Kong and Aotearoa-New Zealand. He will also speak at the Australian Existentialist Society (Melbourne) and the first-ever Colin Wilson conference (Nottingham).

Madeline Reid is a 21-year-old Auckland-based writer. She has been published in *Potroast* and *Debris*. In February 2016 she performed as part of the LGBT Same Same But Different Festival as an up-and-coming writer. She was accepted into the 2016 page stream of the Masters of Creative Writing at IML, with plans to write a novel.

Ron Riddell is a New Zealander who lives in Colombia, South America. A painter, musician and playwright, he has published three novels and more than twenty collections of verse. His website is www.ronriddell.com

Victor Rodger is a New Zealand-born playwright of Samoan and Palagi descent. His first play, *Sons*, won four Chapman Tripp theatre awards, including Best New Play and Best New Writer, while his award-winning play *Black Faggot* has performed to sell-out houses in Melbourne, Brisbane, Edinburgh and New Zealand. A long-time writer for Shortland Street, he is currently adapting *Black Faggot* for the big screen.

Jack Ross is a poet, fiction writer and anthologist, and the editor of *Poetry New Zealand*. He teaches at the Albany Campus of Massey University in Auckland.

L.E. Scott is an African American writer who now lives in Wellington. He has had a number of books published and his work has appeared in many magazines and journals.

Carin Smeaton is an Auckland-based poet. Her book *Tales of the Waihorotiu* is forthcoming from Titus Books in 2016.

Elizabeth Smither is a New Plymouth poet and writer, and a former New Zealand Poet Laureate. Her latest poetry collections are *The Blue Coat* (AUP, 2013) and *Ruby Duby Du* (Cold Hub Press, 2014).

Christina Stachurski has a doctorate in NZ literature from the University of Canterbury, and teaches and researches there. Her plays have been performed around New Zealand. *The Stone Women* is her first novel.

C.K. Stead is the current New Zealand Poet Laureate. His most recent collection of poems is *The Yellow Buoy: Poems 2007–2012*, published by AUP in 2013. He lives in Auckland.

Jillian Sullivan lives in the Ida Valley, Central Otago, where she helped build her straw-bale home. She has published books of poetry, short stories, novels and creative non-fiction.

Ngataiharuru Taepa is currently the Kaihautu Toi Māori Director of Māori Arts at the College of Creative Arts at Massey University in Palmerston North. As an artist, he is known for works that explore traditional kowhaiwhai (rafter painting) forms using modern industrial materials and manufacturing processes.

Leilani Tamu is a poet. In 2013 she was the Fulbright/CreativeNZ Writer in Residence at the University of Hawai`i. Her first book, *The Art of Excavation*, was published in 2014 by Anahera Press.

Rachael Taylor currently works as a teacher-aide, children's art tutor and school holiday programme supervisor, and never stops thinking about stories. She lives with her son in Wellington.

Brian Turner lives in Central Otago. He is a poet and writer, and a former New

Zealand Poet Laureate. His most recent book is *Boundaries: People and places of Central Otago*, published by Penguin-Random House in 2015.

Elizabeth Welsh is a poet and editor from New Zealand, residing in London. She is currently working on her first collection.

Tom Weston lives in Christchurch and works in the legal profession. His latest poetry collection is *Only One Question*, published by Steele Roberts. Of his poem 'The Gift', he writes: 'The island of the poem is Burano, near Venice. Medusa is Italian for jellyfish.'

Mark Young is the editor of *Otoliths*. He grew up in Auckland and now lives in a small town in North Queensland. He has been publishing poetry for more than fifty-five years and his most recent collection, *Bandicoot Habitat*, is just out from Gradient Books of Finland.

CONTRIBUTIONS

Landfall publishes poems, stories, excerpts from works of fiction and non-fiction in progress, reviews, articles on the arts, and portfolios by artists. Written submissions must be typed, with an accurate word count on the last page. Email to landfall@otago.ac.nz with 'Landfall submission' in the subject line, or post to the address below.

Visit our website www.otago.ac.nz/press/landfall/index.html for further information.

SUBSCRIPTIONS

Landfall is published in May and November. The subscription rates for 2016 (two issues) are: New Zealand $50 (including GST); Australia $A52; rest of the world $US53. Sustaining subscriptions help to support New Zealand's longest running journal of arts and letters, and the writers and artists it showcases. These are in two categories: Friend: between $NZ75 and $NZ125 per year. Patron: $NZ250 and above.

Send subscriptions to Otago University Press, PO Box 56, Dunedin, New Zealand. For enquiries, email landfall@otago.ac.nz or call 64 3 479 8807.

Print ISBN: 978-1-927322-23-9
ePDF ISBN: 978-1-927322-64-2
ISSN 00-23-7930

Copyright © Otago University Press 2016

Published by Otago University Press, Level 1, 398 Cumberland Street, Dunedin, New Zealand.

Typeset by Otago University Press.
Printed in New Zealand by Printlink Ltd.

Mango-Tu, Ngataiharuru Taepa, 2013, 1100 x 1100 cm. Earth oxides on plywood.